2 5/19

3 9082 13618 4994

D0801565

Mosquitoes Don't Bite Me

For further information, contact:
Tumblehome Learning, Inc.
201 Newbury St, Suite 201
Boston, MA 02116
http://www.tumblehomelearning.com

Library of Congress Control Number 2017906337
ISBN 978-1-943431-30-4

Noyce, Pendred
Mosquitoes Don't Bite Me / Pendred Noyce - 1st ed

Cover Art: Jan-Willem Boer

Printed in Taiwan

10 9 8 7 6 5 4 3 2 1

Mosquitoes Don't Bite Me

by

Pendred Noyce

TUMBLEHOME l e a r n i n g, Inc.

To my sister Polly,
and to my Kenyan nephews,
Mathew, Danny and Peter.

🦟 one

If I could choose a superpower, I would choose flying. I think my friend Jolene would choose the most beautiful voice in the world, and my uncle Nick would choose a treasure chest that keeps refilling, and my mom would choose—well, that kind of takes the fun out of it, because what my mom would choose is just to walk again.

In my first memory, my father is swinging me around in the air like an airplane. In my memory the green plains are a blur, and zebras on the grassland blend into a smear of stripes, and there's a mountain on one side that comes around again and again. I'm flying, fast and whirling.

My mom says this is a false memory, made of up things I've heard and maybe seen on TV. She says my father used to do that when I was two or three years old, and that's too young for me to remember. And she also says that when we lived in Africa, there were no zebras nearby.

I remember zebras.

Sometimes, on really good nights, I dream I'm flying. This is how I do it. I get running really fast, and then I lean forward and rest myself softly on the air. A breeze lifts me and I'm airborne. My hair billows out as I swoop over the landscape, sometimes over the city but most often over the savannah, where elephants amble and antelope dart. Rivers wind below me, and hippos raise their heads to see me pass. I fly over the land of my ancestors.

The thing is, I do have an actual superpower. At first I hardly noticed it, and I didn't think it was that big a deal, but that was before a lot of people got so excited about it. Sometimes they acted as if there was nothing about me more important than this one simple thing. Still, you probably won't even be that impressed when I tell you.

This is the thing. Mosquitoes don't bite me.

two

*T*he fuss all started with a seventh-grade science project. Our school, which goes from kindergarten through eighth grade, is an art and science magnet school. It's named after Gertrude Elion, a woman who invented lots of really important medicines for leukemia and other sicknesses. She worked at a drug company right here in North Carolina and she even won a Nobel Prize, but she said her biggest rewards were letters from the parents of children she had helped. So of course we're a magnet school for science. But Gertrude also loved the symphony, so after a while they decided to call us a magnet school for the arts too, which is really good for an amazing singer like my best friend Jolene.

My uncle Nick makes fun of our school, calling it the Magnet School for Everything, and he says the school board just called it that to lure in the wealthy parents and make sure the school stayed integrated. I guess it worked, because we're forty percent black, forty percent white, and the rest Asians and Hispanics, except for a few mixed-race kids like me.

Anyway, normally I would team up for a school project with Jolene, but she's in a different science class, and this time Alissa Bowen waved at me from across the room and called out, "Nala, want to be partners?"

I was surprised in a good way. Alissa is pretty and smart and popular, and she definitely comes from one of what Nick would call the "lured-in" families. For some reason lately Alissa seemed to be welcoming me into her group of cool kids. She liked to play with my bracelets and fix my hair and tell me secrets about the teachers. Choosing me as her partner for a science project was a whole new level, though. Alissa had no reason to think I'd be a good partner. I ask a lot of questions in science class, but the rest of the time I fidget and daydream and sometimes even fall asleep.

Our science teacher, Mrs. Garment, has one eyebrow permanently higher than the other, so she always looks skeptical, as if she thinks you might be lying or as if your answer is ridiculous. But this time she didn't ask a question. She just assigned us to confer with our partners about something we could test that would act on the senses of another organism.

I was still trying to figure out what that meant when Alissa said, "I know, let's do mosquitoes. My dad is really into mosquitoes, and there's all this stuff now about the Zika virus. We could test different kinds of mosquito repellants. The only thing is, we'd have to offer our bodies up to science."

I drew back, imagining medical students cutting up my donated corpse. The scalpel hovered over my belly—

Alissa nudged my shoulder. "I mean we'll be the test subjects. We'll get lots of mosquito bites."

I said, "I won't be much help. Mosquitoes don't like me."

"Lucky you. My dad says mosquitoes bite some people more than others."

"Well, they never bite me."

"Oh, you're just exaggerating," Alissa said. "Maybe you don't react that much to the bites. Or maybe you just outrun them."

That was a nice thing for Alissa to say. I run cross-country, but I'm usually only in the middle of the pack.

That afternoon, Jolene and I lingered at the side of the soccer field behind the school. We'd been meeting there a lot lately, because Jolene has a gigantic crush on an eighth-grader named Raymond who plays midfield. When he dribbles the ball, shifting side to side and doing some fancy footwork, the muscles in his legs really stand out and he moves his hands as if he's dancing. I kind of think he's going to break Jolene's heart.

Jolene and I sat on the sideline of soccer practice with our backpacks beside us, painting each other's fingernails even though we'd already painted them a couple of days before. There are only so many things you can do on the sidelines to try and look as if you're not obsessing over some boy. I painted Jolene's nails in red and white stripes, while she tried to paint mine with white stars on a blue background. Very patriotic, but they came out more like polka dots.

Jolene has been my best friend since second grade, ever since I fell on the school driveway playing dodgeball and Jolene took me to the nurse's office. She held my hand as the nurse picked gravel out of my knee. After that we taught each other all the hand-slapping rhymes we knew and spent most of every recess clapping and chanting. Fourth grade was our sock-matching year. Every morning at school we exchanged one sock, so each of us wore unmatched, colorful socks in a mirror image of the other.

"I don't think he even notices me," Jolene said.

"Sure he does."

"If I could just make him feel what I feel."

"You should find out where he lives and sneak up at night to sing under his window. You know, serenade him."

Jolene ignored that suggestion. "I wish there was some secret way to let him know, like a special glow I could give off that only he could see."

"I'm sure he knows how you feel," I said. "I think you're already sending magnetic signals. A person can't not notice that."

"Oh, really?" Jolene asked. "What about you and Tom Vledecky?"

I swiveled to look at Tom in goal. He gave me a quick wave and turned away. I said, "What are you even talking about? I don't have a crush on Tom."

Alissa strolled along the edge of the field until she reached us. She said hi and stood watching us work on our nails. "Very nice," she said, which made me feel self-conscious because I'm pretty sure Alissa has a professional manicure every week.

As we finished, Alissa said, "Nala, I was thinking we could get started on our science project right now, this afternoon."

"Now?" I prefer to procrastinate a bit.

"There are a lot of mosquitoes down by the brook," Alissa said.

The brook runs behind the soccer field, and there's a path down there we train on during cross-country in the fall. That's how I know about mosquitoes not biting me, because the other team members slap and complain, but I don't.

"Want to come too?" Alissa asked Jolene.

Jolene stood, dusted her hands, and shook her head. She doesn't approve of my new friendship with Alissa. She thinks I'm being seduced by how rich Alissa is. On weekends, Alissa supposedly hosts great pool parties where the girls slip down a water slide and eat fancy sandwiches and practice dance moves on the pool deck afterward. Sometimes over winter break she takes a friend skiing with her in the Rocky Mountains, and once she even took Elizabeth Salley to Paris. I mean, who wouldn't be seduced by a chance like that? I never get to go anywhere.

"Well, then," Alissa said, corralling me with an arm around my shoulder and pulling me away from Jolene, "this is our control run. We walk through the woods along the brook path with no mosquito repellant on and count how many bites we get. That will be our baseline. Now check the time. We walk for ten minutes."

We checked the time on our cell phones. Three twenty-two.

It was already warm for April in Durham, North Carolina, so both of us wore short sleeves. As we meandered along the path, Alissa kept squealing and slapping herself, but I half-floated along thinking how awesome it would be to fly low along the brook, dipping over the rhododendron bushes and winding among the trees.

After a few hundred yards, way before the ten minutes were up, Alissa yelled, "I can't stand this!" She scuffled through the underbrush and scrambled up the bank, knocking off a bunch of chokecherry blossoms, until she could cross the road to the sidewalk on the far side. There she whirled around, flapping her arms to clear the cloud of mosquitoes hovering over her. "What we do for science!" she said. "I must have about forty bites. How about you?"

"None," I said.

Alissa glared at me as if she'd caught me cheating.

"I told you," I reminded her.

She let out a little disgusted breath of air, "Puh! Well, this project obviously isn't going to work."

"I told you," I said again. When she didn't answer, I offered, "You could do the experiment and I could count your bites and write down the data."

"You mean I do all the suffering and you get half the credit? No way." Alissa stuck out her lower lip. "I'll have to come up with another idea. See you tomorrow." And she pivoted and was gone.

Alissa can be abrupt like that. It keeps her friends on their toes. I was pretty sure she wasn't really mad at me. I mean, it wasn't my fault mosquitoes don't like me. Like my light-brown skin, my flat chest and wiry, dark brown hair, like Alissa's blond hair and cream-colored skin and perfect figure, I figured our different attractiveness to mosquitoes was just something we were born with.

three

When I got home, my uncle Nick stood in the driveway, oiling the gears of his bicycle, which was balanced upside down on the asphalt in front of him. Nick is my mom's youngest brother, and he's closer to my age than hers. My mom and I live in the downstairs apartment so she can get around easily in her wheelchair, and Nick lives in the upstairs apartment for now. He's twenty-two, and he's living with us to save money while he goes to college part time. Even though he's smart, he's not that serious about studying. "Steve Jobs didn't finish college," he says. "Neither did Bill Gates." Uncle Nick wants to get rich, but he doesn't like computers, which is a problem, because it seems like computers are the main way people get rich nowadays.

While he figures out how to get rich, Nick works at the Whole Foods Market in Durham, and he also helps out my mom and me.

Nick wiped the bicycle chain with a rag as he turned the pedals. "Your mom called. She said to turn the oven to four hundred and put the chicken in to roast."

My mom works at the town library. She can do everything but reach the highest shelves, so she gets tall patrons to help her shelve books that have to go up high. For some reason, people really like doing this. I think helping my mom put books away is an easy way for them to feel like good people.

I placed my hands on my hips. "And why can't you put in the chicken, Mister Macho Man?"

Nick tipped his head and grinned at me. "Actually, I did. I'm just pulling your chain. But your mom was curious about why you weren't home yet."

"Because I was working on a science project, that's why." I hadn't told my mom about how Jolene and I were stalking the soccer team.

"Hey, don't snap at me. I'm not the one who worries every moment you're out of sight."

I decided to change the subject. "Nick, do mosquitoes bite you?"

"Of course they do. I'm human, and I'm delicious."

"Well, they don't bite me."

Nick righted his bicycle and rolled it back and forward a little. "Huh. Well, you should bottle that. You'd make a million."

"I just thought it might be something that runs in the family."

"Like our beautiful wavy blond hair?" Nick asked, pretending to primp. Nick, of course, like my mom and all my North Carolina relatives, is white. "Not on our side," Nick said. "Maybe that comes from your African side."

Because my mom and I left Kenya when I was three, I don't really know the African side of my family. Sometimes when I Skype my dad, a bunch of my African cousins pop in and out of the background. And in an album my mom keeps on a medium-high shelf in her bedroom, there are photos from her wedding. I like to look at the one of my father's tiny old grandmother perched on a stiff chair with her tall, skinny husband, my great-grandfather, standing behind her. Both of them have a fluff of gray hair around their heads, like unpolished haloes. I closed my eyes and tried to remember if I'd ever met my great-grandparents in real life. I couldn't remember. They were like those cut-out silhouettes you sometimes see, black and blank, just another hole in the African part of me.

"Hey, Nala, come back," Nick said.

"What does it feel like when a mosquito bites you?" I asked.

"It sucks," Nick said, and he laughed.

four

The next day, Alissa started bragging about me at lunch. "Nala has a superpower. Mosquitoes don't bite her."

Tom put down his fork and gazed at me. "Hey, you could grow up to be a forest ranger or something."

"That's random," I said.

Tom is nice, and Jolene says he's a really great goalkeeper, and he has wavy hair like Uncle Nick's, but he wears it too long and he's way too tall for himself and kind of goofy. Also, he has pimples, which I know I shouldn't care about because they're literally only skin deep and besides he'll outgrow them. I can't figure out why Tom likes to sit with us girls. He fumbled with his milk carton. "Like, I mean, the mosquitoes would never drive you crazy. You could just really enjoy yourself. You know, sit by a lake and watch the sunset and stuff."

Elizabeth, who sat right next to Alissa, piped up, "I bet it's because Nala has dark skin."

Jolene, who is much darker than I am and gets offended easily, leaned from my other side across the table toward Elizabeth. "What's that supposed to mean?"

Elizabeth should have been careful what she said next. But she went blithely on: "Black skin is, you know, thicker. Maybe the mosquitoes can't get through."

Jolene slammed her hand on the table. "That is the most ignorant thing I've heard all week. A million Africans die of malaria every year. Those are black people. And malaria, in case you didn't know, comes from mosquito bites."

After a while with nobody saying anything, Tom spoke up. "Um, anybody going to the Killers concert?" Like I said, Tom is nice.

That night, while I was washing the dinner dishes and handing them down to my mother to dry, I asked her, "Do people really die of malaria?"

"That came out of the blue," she said. "Why are you thinking about malaria?"

"Jolene said it kills like a million people a year," I said, with a little laugh to show I knew that was an exaggeration.

"Close enough," my mom said. "Mostly in Africa, some in Asia. A lot of them are children." She said this calmly, while drying a plate. My mother has long, golden-brown hair that falls to cover her shoulders in shining waves. She's grown sort of chubby from sitting in a wheelchair day after day. She's calm and cheerful most of the time, but sometimes she says she misses the days when she had adventures.

I asked her, "What happens when you get malaria?"

Before her accident, my mom was a nurse in Kenya, in East Africa, where I was born. She said, "People with malaria get high fevers that come and go. They can get a headache and body aches and anemia, which means their red blood cells are bursting apart. Then, if it's really bad, the malaria parasites get to the brain and the patient has seizures."

"Do we have malaria around here?"

Mom turned her wheelchair around so she could look me straight in the eye. "Sometimes a traveler comes home with malaria, but we don't have the kind of mosquito that carries the parasite from one person to another. You don't have to worry, honey."

I took the plate from her and put it away. "I'm not worried. I could even go to Africa and not worry. You know how mosquitoes don't bite me."

Mom ignored the part about going to Africa the way she always does. She doesn't fly since the accident, so unless we spend a few weeks on a huge cruise ship that can cross the ocean and then loop down around the bottom of the African continent, which is called the Cape of Good Hope, we're never going back to Kenya, which sometimes makes me want to cry. It's funny to be homesick for a place you hardly remember. I closed my eyes and wondered if, even in my dreams, I could fly as far as Kenya.

"Do people in my family get malaria?" I asked. "Did Dad, or any of my cousins? Did you, when we lived there?"

Mom shook her head. "We were always very careful. We wore long clothes and slept under mosquito nets."

"Well, anyway, I want to write to Dad," I said. And after I finished the dishes I went into the study and turned on the computer.

Hey, Dad, I wrote.

There's this weird thing about me. Mosquitoes don't bite me. Do they bite you? Does this run in the family?

School is going okay.

Love, Nala.

The next morning, I got Dad's reply before I went to school.

Good morning, Nala, my little lioness. It is true, some people in our family, including me, are so strong even the mosquitoes are afraid of us! Also, in our part of the country, there grows a plant that, when you rub it on your skin, keeps the mosquitoes away. But it protects only our people. People from other tribes have tried it and it does not work for them.

Much love,

Your father.

five

That day, Alissa rushed up to me at lunch. "Guess what!" she said, actually forgetting to take her place at the head of the table and instead plopping her tray down next to mine. "I couldn't wait to tell you. My dad wants to meet you."

Jolene, already sitting across from me, snorted. "And who's your dad to get us all excited? The governor or something?"

Alissa flipped her ponytail from one shoulder to the other. "He's the president of Drossila. You know, Drossila Pharmaceuticals? They make all these important medicines for things like infections and brain disease."

"So your pops is a drug dealer," Jolene said.

Alissa glared at her.

I asked in a small voice, "Why does he want to meet me?"

"Because mosquitoes don't bite you! Drossila's funding a big mosquito study at the university. You must put out some secret ingredient from your skin, and my dad says if they can figure out what it is, well, that could be really important."

"You mean for the million people who get malaria?" I asked. That was my very quiet way of standing up for Jolene, who knows things.

"Well, and Zika. Zika is a really big deal right now. You know, the virus that makes babies get born with small heads? Anyway, my dad wants to know if he can call and talk to your parents."

"Um, sure, I guess so. To my mom."

"Don't do it," Jolene said.

I gave her a look that said, *You don't own me*, and turned my chair toward Alissa. "I'll text you our phone number."

"Got it." Alissa pulled out a chair to sit down, but then, seeming to feel the heat of Jolene glowering at her, wavered, picked up her tray, wiggled the fingers of one hand to say, "See you later," and started a group at another table.

Jolene watched her go and then leaned across the table toward me. "Haven't you ever heard of Henrietta Lacks?"

"Sure, of course I have," I lied.

"Well, don't let them get their hooks in you, that's all."

That night, Nick and I made the dinner salad together. While I was deciding whether to chop the tomatoes into wedges or little wagon wheels, I asked him who Henrietta Lacks was.

"Henrietta Lacks was a poor black woman in Baltimore who got a terrible cancer," he said. "She died from it, but the doctors who treated her took some of her cancer cells to use in their lab. The cells just kept growing and growing, and soon these docs were selling her cells to other people."

"People buy cells?"

"Only really special cells. These ones last forever, because of the cancer she had. Scientists from all over the world are still using Henrietta's cells in their experiments. Everybody calls them HeLa cells, and they're famous in biology."

"So why would Jolene warn me about Henrietta Lacks?" I asked, and I told him about our lunch conversation.

"Hoo-ee," he said. "Your Jolene sounds pretty fierce. But she has a point. Nobody asked Henrietta Lacks if they could use her cells. Nobody paid her for them."

"How could they? You said she died."

"Nobody paid her family. They acted as if they owned her cells from the beginning. Listen, Nala, I told you this mosquito thing means you might be sitting on a million bucks. Say Alissa's dad gets some chemical from your sweat or something and puts it in a million cans of mosquito repellant."

"Yeah, right," I said. "Like my sweat would fill a million cans. Besides, Grandma Ronnie says only horses sweat. Men perspire. Ladies gleam."

Nick rolled his eyes and dumped a pile of chopped cucumber into the salad bowl. "The point is, you have to demand your fair share. A dollar a bottle, and you pay off your mom's house and pay for your college—"

"And your college too, I bet you're thinking."

"Naturally." Nick patted me on the head. "I'll be your agent."

I thought about what I'd do with a million dollars. I'd take flying lessons, that was one thing. I'd fly my dad and grandparents and aunts and uncles and cousins over from Kenya for a vacation, and we'd visit Yellowstone and the Grand Canyon.

"Are you two finished in there?" Mom called. "Can you take out the meat loaf?"

"I bet nothing happens, and Alissa's dad won't even call," I said, as I sprinkled dressing over the salad.

But Mr. Bowen did call, after dinner. My mom answered, and she echoed parts of the conversation, like, "Oh yes, I know Alissa," and "Drossila, you say?" She kept raising her eyebrows at me in a questioning way, and each time I shrugged as if to say, "Whatever." Still, Uncle Nick's million dollars were doing hip-hop in my head, so when Mom passed me the phone, my hands shook a little.

"Hello," I said.

"This is Steve Bowen, Alissa's dad," a deep and pleasant voice said on the other end of the line. "I was just asking your mother if you'd like to come with Alissa to visit a lab one day after school next week."

"Uh, sure, what kind of lab?" I asked. Across the room, Uncle Nick waved his arms and pointed to himself, trying to get my attention.

"We're sponsoring some very interesting research on flies and mosquitoes at the university," Mr. Bowen said. "Have you heard of odorant receptors? No, of course you haven't. They're the little receptors that tell us what things smell like. Mosquitoes have lots of them."

I tried to picture a mosquito's nose.

"You'll like Daniel Wright, who runs the lab," Mr. Bowen said. "Dr. Daniel Wright. He's African American."

I wondered why he added that detail. Maybe Mr. Bowen knew about Henrietta Lacks too, and figured I'd trust a black scientist more. Maybe he was right.

"Okay," I said. "I mean, yes, please, that sounds like fun."

"Your mother is invited too, of course," Mr. Bowen said.

Nick was still waving his arms. I sighed. "How about if I bring my uncle instead?"

six

The next Tuesday afternoon, Uncle Nick rode his bike to meet Alissa and me when school got out. When Alissa saw him, she smoothed down her hair and re-applied her lip gloss. I suppose my uncle really is kind of handsome, but still, the way Alissa was primping bothered me.

Nick locked his bike on the bike rack and released one wheel to carry with him. He does that to make extra sure no one steals his bike.

"So this is Alissa," he said, sticking out his hand to shake hers.

I swear she batted her eyelids at him.

He asked, "Is it true your old man runs Drossila? Looks like it's doing really well in the stock market right now. How'd he get into that line of business anyway?"

Uncle Nick is always trying to slip in some way of asking how rich people got rich. To distract him, I said, "I bet this is our car."

A sleek black Cadillac pulled up in the school's circular driveway, and a distinguished-looking man stepped out. He had a charcoal gray suit, a red tie, and silvery, perfectly groomed hair. I glanced at Alissa, who nodded, so I stepped forward and bravely stuck out my hand. "Good afternoon, Mr. Bowen. I'm Nala."

The silvery man laughed and opened the back door for me. "I'm just the driver," he said.

Nick, chuckling, scooted into the back seat after me, while Alissa took the front passenger seat. I stuck my tongue out at Nick and turned toward the window with my cheeks burning.

Less than ten minutes later, the driver dropped us at the back entrance of a university laboratory building. Waiting for us stood a buff, youngish, medium-tall black man wearing a lab coat with a bright orange and yellow sun embroidered on its pocket. His long hair hung to his shoulders in about a hundred braids, and he had a little beard sticking off his chin like the statues of King Tut. This time I made no assumptions before he introduced himself as Dr. Daniel Wright, head of the fly lab. "Call me Daniel," he said.

"So, how'd you get interested in this line of work?" Uncle Nick asked as we trailed Daniel up the stairs to the fourth floor. This time Nick's interest surprised me, because Daniel Wright didn't look rich; the soles of his basketball shoes were peeling away, so they sort of flip-flopped as he climbed.

"Fruit fly experiments in high school biology," Daniel answered. He turned back to grin at us. "Red or white eyes, wings that were curly or straight, a gazillion tiny flies crawling around—somehow it just caught me."

He led us down the hall and into a room that looked like a cleaner, shinier copy of the labs I've seen at the high school. Those special metal chimneys called hoods lined the outer walls, and sinks and long black counters spanned the room in neat ranks.

Various men and women who looked like Nick's age or a little older bent silently over computers or examined bits of film against a light board. Normally, I would space out in a place like this. I mean, adults at work—what shouts out "Boring!" more than that? But for some reason, whether it was the excitement in Daniel's voice or the thought of a million people dying of malaria—anyway, for some reason I paid attention. Alissa was the one who wrapped strands of her very straight blond hair around her finger and sighed a lot.

Daniel took us to the fruit fly room straightaway. Fruit flies, trapped in large jars, flew to the top of the jars or crawled around the bottom. Daniel tapped the glass, showing us flies that couldn't fly, flies that only turned to the right, flies with red eyes, flies with yellow eyes. A few escaped flies swarmed around our heads and a couple of dead ones lay on the floor. Daniel showed us a fly under a microscope. Its eye looked like someone had wrapped a black window screen around a tennis ball. The eye stared up at me, alien and robotic.

Next we visited the mosquito room. The mosquitoes hummed around inside glass boxes about twice the size of toasters. Each box had a hole in one side with a long white cloth sleeve coming off it. "We stick our hands through here," Daniel explained, "and count the bites we get. Anyone want to try?"

Nick shuffled his feet, and Alissa shook her head. Daniel raised his eyebrows in my direction.

"Sure," I said. But my stomach wobbled as I stepped up. This seemed very official. What if my special effect on mosquitoes didn't work in the laboratory? I would disappoint Daniel, and Mr. Bowen would figure he'd wasted company money on our limousine.

"Just rinse your hand first," Daniel said, pointing to a sink.

Did he think I was cheating, wearing Deep Woods Off or something to trick him? I narrowed my eyes at him as I rinsed and dried my hands. But he just smiled at me.

After hesitating a moment in front of the glass mosquito box, I threaded my arm into the sleeve. Where the sleeve met the box, I had to squeeze my hand through a kind of cuff, which closed around my wrist, not letting any insects escape. What happened next was completely not dramatic. The mosquitoes kept flying around the box, and none of them landed on my hand.

Daniel leaned close, almost pressing his nose against the glass. "Fascinating," he said. "Let's see if you can last a minute." He pointed to a clock on the wall. We all watched the second hand go around, and then he nodded at me, and I pulled my arm out.

"How do we know there's not something wrong with your mosquitoes?" Nick asked.

"Always better to check," Daniel said. He folded back the sleeve of his lab coat and pushed his arm into the box. Immediately several mosquitoes landed. "Look at them," he said. "Bloodthirsty little buggers. Watch their fat little bellies turn red with my blood. Do you know if you cut one little sensory nerve from their stomach to their brain, they'll keep sucking blood until they burst? All right, girls, that's enough." He shook his hand so the mosquitoes rose before he pulled his arm out of the sleeve. "Can't squish any of these valuable experimental animals," he explained.

"Why do you call them girls?" I asked.

"Only female mosquitoes suck blood. They do it to get protein for laying eggs. Males stick to nectar."

Alissa volunteered, "I slapped about a hundred valuable experimental animals down by the brook, and I'm not even sorry."

Daniel laughed and led us out of the mosquito room. "So here's the deal," he said. "A number of research groups have studied odorant receptors in fruit flies and now mosquitoes. We're trying to understand how and what they smell. And then on the other side we look at people. Some people attract lots of mosquitoes and some not nearly so many. We know carbon dioxide is one compound that draws them in."

"Wait," Nick said. "Carbon dioxide is the gas we breathe out with every breath we take."

"That's right. All animals exhale air enriched in carbon dioxide, so that's one way mosquitoes sense their prey."

"You mean if I hold my breath mosquitoes won't bite me?" Alissa asked.

Daniel smiled at her. "That depends. How long can you hold your breath?"

Alissa opened her mouth but didn't answer. Instead, she closed her mouth and wrapped a strand of hair around her finger.

Daniel said, "Sometimes bacteria on our skin carry a certain smell to mosquitoes that they either like or don't like."

"You mean I might be covered in stinky germs?" I asked, kind of shrinking into myself. Maybe my superpower was really disgusting.

"Not stinky to us," Daniel said. "People might not be able to smell them at all. Or it could be some other kind of chemical your skin puts out. We're all a little different. We each have a smell profile that's a little different. Think of how bloodhounds are able to track criminals or lost children."

I imagined a bloodhound nosing along the ground after me as I fled through some forest.

"We try to find out what molecules attract or repel mosquitoes," Daniel went on. "The way smell works is that certain compounds get airborne and travel to our noses, or to bloodhounds' noses, or to smell receptors in the antennae of mosquitoes or other insects."

"Gross," Alissa said. "Does that mean when we smell garbage, tiny pieces of garbage are floating into our noses?"

"Sort of."

"I guess that's why people wear perfume," I said.

"I don't get it," Alissa said.

"So molecules of perfume float away instead of molecules of the person herself." I know molecules are small, but still I imagined more and more of me turning into smell, leaving a faded ghost behind, like poor dead Henrietta Lacks. Jolene's warnings were really getting into my head.

Daniel laughed as if I'd made a clever joke. He said, "Dogs and mosquitoes have much more sensitive smell receptors than we do. They pick up scents we don't even notice."

I thought about this. "If we can't smell it, how you can find out what I smell like to a mosquito?"

"Good question. Remember, the smell is carried by certain molecules, very small amounts of chemicals. We can use some chemical techniques, like gas chromatography and mass spectrometry, to figure out the difference between your smells and those of other people."

I repeated, "Gas chrome? Mass something? What are those?"

Alissa raised her hand to cover a fake yawn.

Daniel noticed. He said to me, "I could show you some of that next time, if you'd like to come back. And if you're willing, when you come back I'd like to try and collect some of your, let's call them emanations. Your smells." He explained how he would do that.

I liked Daniel, and I liked being singled out as special, but Jolene's voice still shouted warnings in my head. I couldn't get Henrietta Lacks out of my mind, how they scraped away her cells and let them grow as she died a painful death. Maybe to Daniel and Mr. Bowen I was just a sack of smells. "Is it important?" I asked.

Daniel scratched his head. "I'll tell you the truth. I've never seen someone as unwelcoming to mosquitoes as you are. You may be one of a kind."

Before I could agree, Nick broke in. "Will you pay her?" Nick liked to say that anything can be a business negotiation.

"I was just getting to that. I think I can swing twenty-five dollars an hour for a volunteer subject. We have some paperwork for her parents to sign." He looked at Nick. "We're interested in other family members too, as long as they're willing to leave their arm in the mosquito box for a minute."

"Will you want to test us even if mosquitoes like to bite us?"

"We need people to compare Nala to."

Nick considered. "Well, I hate mosquitoes, but the pay sure beats Whole Foods. Sign me up."

seven

In the end, four of us came back to the lab. My grandmother Ronnie had decided to visit for the weekend, and she insisted on coming along. Ronnie's full name is Veronica, and she's fifty-nine. She plays tennis and swims and can be fun when she's not in her dramatic mode, but she gets tragic and protective around my mother.

This time, instead of a silver-haired chauffeur picking us up in a limo, my mother drove her special van. She rolled her wheelchair onto a lift, which elevated her to where she could wheel into the driver's space, and then she used hand levers to drive. Daniel had instructed us not to eat any garlic or wear any perfume or deodorant for a couple of days before we came. He had also asked us to wear the same pair of nylon socks for two whole days.

I sat in the back next to Nick. Even without deodorant, and even though he'd been biking a lot, I didn't think he smelled too bad.

Daniel met us at the back door of the university lab again. He was extra nice to my mom, the way people sometimes are, and he offered to push her wheelchair. "I can handle it," my mom said in her grumpy voice. So Daniel just led us all to the elevator.

Then, when we entered the lab, a surprise: Alissa sat in a swivel chair, turning it from side to side. "I didn't know you were coming," I said, and I introduced her to my mother and grandmother.

"What did you think?" Alissa asked. "This is going to be the best science project ever."

"Wait, so are you getting tested too?"

"No, why would I? I'm not the one with the amazing superpower of frightening mosquitoes away."

I thought about this while Daniel showed my mother and Ronnie around the lab. In my mind, this mosquito thing was no longer just a science project, and Alissa and I weren't the ones doing it. Besides, I was pretty sure I didn't want our whole class talking about how I had a weird smell. "I thought you wanted us to do a different project. I was thinking we could do something more normal. Like, you know how certain plants turn toward the light? I thought we could grow a bean plant in a dark closet with a blue light on one side and a red one on the other side, and see which way it turns."

Alissa spun in her chair and waved her hand. "Been done before. But discovering a brand new mosquito repellant coming off your skin, that's new."

"But it's my skin," I said. "I'm not Henrietta Lacks."

"Who's that?" Alissa asked. "Look, this is a really good deal. Daniel helps us with all this fancy equipment, and we make a snazzy poster and score an A." She gave me a dazzling smile.

Before I could think of an answer, Daniel came back and asked me to put my arm in the mosquito box again. Actually, he asked all of us, and everyone did except Alissa. This is how many bites we got in a minute: Nick 32, Ronnie 30, Mom 24, me 0. Alissa typed it all into Daniel's computer. Then Daniel asked us to hand over our dirty socks.

Ronnie said to Nick, "I can't believe there's someone actually willing to touch your socks."

Daniel laughed. "Mosquitoes love smelly feet. Especially malaria mosquitoes. In fact, some people are experimenting with using smelly old socks to trap malaria mosquitoes."

So we all took off and donated our socks and then put on fresh ones my mother had brought along. But that wasn't the end of our body smells. "It's good to check more than one way," Daniel said. He took us into another room to see a giant bag attached by tubes to some air pumps. It looked like one of those oven bags, kind of plastic and silvery at the same time. The idea was we would climb inside the bag and air would be pumped past our skin and collected. Daniel would turn up the heat in the room so various smelly molecules would evaporate from our skin and get captured.

Mom volunteered to go first. Nick lifted her out of her wheelchair, and Daniel slid the bag over her legs. Then they wrestled it up around her and settled her on a chair. At that point I sent the others out of the room and helped my mother scoot her dress out from under her seat and up off her shoulders. That way no one but me would catch a glimpse of her underwear. The more skin exposed to the air, Daniel told us, the better.

I pulled the drawstring gently closed around my mother's neck and called Daniel back. Daniel closed the door of her glass chamber.

"It's going to get pretty warm in here," Daniel said. "You might want to wait in the other room where there are chairs."

I checked with my mom to see if she wanted me to stay, but she used her chin to wave me away.

In the waiting room, Nick settled down to look at a motorcycle magazine.

I asked Ronnie, "Why do you think Mom only got twenty-four bites?"

Nick looked up from his magazine. "Maybe she picked up some kind of resistance in Kenya. How long was she there?"

"Five and a half years," Ronnie said, before I could answer. "Five years and five months healthy, one month broken." And then she said under her breath, "I hate that place."

I thought I saw Alissa's ears perk up. She leaned in. "Why?"

"It's not Africa's fault, Mom," Uncle Nick said. He put his magazine up in front of his face, because he could tell she was about to go tragic on us.

"Africa, Africa, so romantic," Ronnie said. "Weren't there enough poor sick people to take care of here in America?"

"What do you mean?" Alissa asked.

Ronnie had just been waiting for a new chance to tell the story. When Nick was just a little kid, my mom studied to be a nurse, and as soon as she could, she signed up for a tour of duty in Kenya. She worked with the Flying Doctors who flew into villages to do checkups and give vaccines and bring sick people back to the capital. It was in the Flying Doctors that she met my father.

"Flying Doctors," I murmured. It had always sounded perfect to me.

"Your dad's a doctor?" Alissa asked me.

I shook my head. "The doctors didn't fly the planes. My father was a pilot."

"Janet brought him home to meet the family," Ronnie said. "And we were very nice to him, weren't we, Nick?" She turned to Alissa. "But then they got married and he took her away!" She pulled out a tissue. Uncle Nick sighed, set down his magazine, and slid over to put his arm around his mother's shoulders.

This is why my mom doesn't always look forward to visits from Ronnie. At least this time my grandmother was going to have her cry while my mom snuggled in her giant oven bag in the next room.

Alissa looked back and forth from Ronnie to me. Her eyes glittered. I couldn't help feeling she was gathering up great gossip to share with her friends. I missed Jolene, who usually just grunted when I told her things about my family, but somehow let me know she'd keep them private.

"My parents flew all over Kenya," I told Alissa. "They saw the wildebeest migration and the coast where the blue ocean meets the golden sand." Those were my mother's words. My mother likes to tell me about those flights.

I hoped my grandmother would leave it there, but she didn't. "If she had just stayed home taking care of you," Ronnie said in my direction.

"She had her work, Ma," Nick said. "Janet was devoted to her work."

I said, "I loved staying with my Aunt Eliza." This was probably true, because my parents have told me my dad's little sister, who was about sixteen and very small, used to haul me around everywhere in a toy wagon or on her hip, to the market to play with the fat, yellow-green papayas or into the backyard to chase chickens. They said I laughed and chattered all the time. I just don't remember it.

"And then your father let your mother fly as a passenger with a bumbling, incompetent..." Ronnie broke down, sobbing into her tissue.

"Christ," said Nick. "Do you have to do this every time? Do you think it's fair to Nala?"

"What happened?" Alissa asked. She leaned toward Ronnie, her mouth slightly open.

"A plane crash," Nick said.

What happened is this: The plane hit the ground hard and then suddenly swerved on the rutted runway and struck a cinderblock building. The pilot and the doctor in the front seat died in the crash. My mother was in the back seat, and when she was thrown forward against the seat belt, her spine snapped. Somehow, the villagers got her out of the plane and radioed for help. My father flew the plane that came to rescue her. "I could hardly even see through my tears," my dad told me once on Skype. "I don't know how I ever landed."

Ronnie sobbed. "My baby was paralyzed," she wailed, reaching for Alissa's hand. Alissa pulled her hand away just out of Ronnie's reach.

A month after the accident, my mother rode in an air ambulance back to the States. It took all her savings, all Ronnie's savings. Ronnie carried the three-year-old me in her arms. My father couldn't get a visa. He stood waving out the airport window, tears in his eyes. I feel as if I can remember looking back at him, and at my little Aunt Eliza by his side.

Telling this story, Ronnie wept, while Nick, his jaw set, patted her shoulder. I sat hunched in my chair, wondering why, if my mom could move on and so could I, my grandmother had to be so dramatic.

That's when Daniel knocked and stuck his head in the door. "Who's next?"

 **eight**

A few days later, Uncle Nick called me out of the closet where I had set up my bean plants and colored lights.

"It's Daniel Wright on the phone," Nick said. "He wants to talk to you." Nick wiggled his eyebrows at me as he handed over the phone.

Daniel said, "I'm happy to tell you we have very promising results. It seems there are three or maybe four compounds you give off from your skin that your mother, uncle, and grandmother do not."

The news made me feel weird. Daniel sounded somehow proud of me, but I hadn't done anything except give him my dirty socks and sit in a garbage bag.

"Um, good, I guess," I said. "Does that mean Drossila will be able to make a new insect repellant?"

"Maybe someday, but it's not that straightforward. For one thing, we've found these compounds, these chemicals, but we haven't characterized them."

"Speak English," I said.

He laughed. "Until we work out their chemical structure, we can't make more of them for ourselves. Not only that, we don't even know which of these compounds is the important one."

"Oh." That was disappointing. Maybe my superpower wouldn't save a million children after all. Though come to think of it, why didn't they just use the insect repellants we already have?

"What we need," Daniel continued, "is more study subjects."

"What do you mean?"

"Well, your ability to fend off mosquitoes must be genetic. It must come from somewhere. If not from your mother, it must come from your father. I'm hoping you can help me persuade him to come in."

"My father lives in Africa," I told him. "I haven't seen him since I was three years old."

Now it was Daniel's turn to sound disappointed. "Oh."

I thought about how I liked that he had called to talk to me. Me, not Nick or my mom. As if I was really an important part of this project.

"I talk to my dad all the time," I offered. "I've got loads of cousins and things. And my dad says mosquitoes don't like our family very much."

"That's important news," Daniel said. "You know, this interests me very much, scientifically. It sounds like your family has evolved some kind of resistance to mosquito bites." He thought for a moment. "Are you sure your father has no other family members in the States?"

"I'm pretty sure. I never heard of any. I can ask. But maybe you could get them to send you some blood samples or something."

"No," Daniel said sadly. "I need the bite test and the chemical collector. We won't find anything helpful in their blood."

Then a little hope began to quiver inside me. "What if you ask Mr. Bowen to help you? What if he gets a special visa and brings my dad over to help with your research? Oh, please, that would be such a good idea, Alissa would get an A plus on her science project for sure, tell him that!"

Daniel laughed softly. "You are a good salesperson, Nala. I will carry your message to Mr. Bowen and see what we can do."

Frogs jumped around inside my stomach. My dad might be coming. He might actually be coming. All at once I loved Alissa and her mysterious father.

nine

Alissa had the idea of making me run around the gym and shoot baskets until the perspiration dripped off of me. Then she wiped me down with a towel and wiped the towel all over herself, holding her nose and wincing as she did so. She made me take pictures on my phone "to document our method." She even slung the sweaty towel around her neck for extra protection. Then we walked out to the edge of the soccer field, past Jolene who had actually resorted to doing math homework on the sidelines. Jolene glared at me, but Alissa suggested I wait there too while she, Alissa, took a stroll along the brook, to see if the odor of my sweat kept mosquitoes away.

"Shouldn't I come with you?" I asked.

"If the mosquitoes have a choice of biting you or me, they'll always bite me," she said. "But with a choice of biting me or nothing, maybe they'll choose nothing."

I wasn't sure that made sense, but I sat on the grass beside Jolene and pulled out my math book.

"So buddy-buddy," Jolene said. "Has she asked you to a pool party yet?"

"You're just jealous," I said. "And also a grouch."

Jolene said, "Elizabeth told me Raymond brought a girl from another school to last Friday's dance."

MOSQUITOES DON'T BITE ME

I thought about what to say. "He obviously has bad taste."

"You're right," Jolene said. "So what am I doing here?" She slammed her math book shut and stood, but I could see her wavering.

"Math?" I offered.

"That's right. Pre-Algebra, chapter fourteen." Jolene sat down again and bent over the book.

A moment later, Alissa was back. She jogged over to us, waving her hand. "Three bites! I only got three bites!"

I stood slowly. I hadn't mentioned to Alissa that I was going ahead with the experiment about whether bean plants turn to blue or red light. Explaining why I felt weird about the mosquito experiment was just too hard. Mostly, I told myself, it was because bringing the university fly lab in on our project felt like cheating. Anyway, now Alissa had a real result of our own, so I decided to be a good sport.

"We should get some other kids to try it too," I said. "We need a sample size larger than one."

"No, I don't think so," Alissa said.

"Why not?"

"I don't want to bother. Besides, who would do it?"

That was strange. I was pretty sure Alissa could talk half our class into doing anything she wanted.

"Come on," I said. "Elizabeth. Tom. Jolene would do it if I asked her. Wouldn't you, Jolene."

"No," Jolene said.

Alissa rolled her eyes at me. "I know you think Tom Vledecky has a crush on you but I don't think even he wants to get wiped down in your sweat. That's just gross."

I recoiled as if she had slapped me. Before I could think of something cutting to say, Alissa swiveled and walked away. Like I said, she does that sometimes. But this time, the notion struck me that she was trying to escape something. Escape what? Someone else seeing our experiment?

I chased after her. "Why don't you want anyone else to try my sweat? Wait a minute, why didn't you even want me to come along and see it?"

Alissa walked faster. I reached for her shoulder to make her turn and face me. "You didn't really do it, did you? You didn't go along the whole path!"

She jerked away from me. "Who even cares? Don't you see we have a great story?"

"But you're..." I couldn't bring myself to say right out she was lying. "You're... making up data!"

"Just shut up," she told me.

 **ten**

When I returned to Jolene, who was still squinting at her math book, and told her I thought Alissa was making up results for our science project she just said, "I warned you not to let that girl exploit you."

"Who said anything about exploiting me? The problem is she's cheating!" I plopped down beside Jolene and asked, "Do you think I should tell?"

I expected Jolene to say yes, of course I should tell, but she surprised me. "Are you sure you can prove it? Because if you can't, she'll crush you, and everyone will call you a liar. You won't get anywhere. Who are people going to listen to, you or Alissa?"

I kept that in mind the next afternoon when I went to talk to Mrs. Garment after school. "I want to change my science project," I said. "I'd like to work on something alone."

Mrs. Garment gazed at me with her one skeptical eyebrow raised. "Do you have a good reason?"

I hesitated. "I just think the experiment could be run in a better way."

"Then it's your responsibility to make that happen. Scientists collaborate, Nala. A big part of your grade on this project will be based on how well you and your partner work as a team."

The next day, I caught Alissa after science class and tried to talk her into repeating the towel experiment with other people. I even suggested she should run around the gym and let me wipe *her* sweat on *me* to see what happened with the mosquitoes.

"No way," Alissa said. "I don't like to sweat. It enlarges the pores. Listen, if you want to do more, why don't you just make a poster about malaria? I think, with what we've already done, that would really nail us an A."

Because of the bad feeling at the pit of my stomach, I decided that afternoon to call Daniel at the lab. My hands got damp as the phone rang, because I wasn't sure he'd really want to talk to me. Maybe I was like Henrietta Lacks, only as important to the scientists as the pieces of her they wanted to study.

"Daniel Wright here," he answered.

"It's Nala," I said.

"Hey, I was hoping you would call. I promised to show you gas chromatography and HPLC. You want to come down to the lab?"

"Uh, sure. But it's not that. I need some advice." I hesitated, uncertain how he would take me bad-mouthing the daughter of his sponsor. "What would you do if you were working on an experiment with someone, say another scientist, and you began to think they were making up data?"

There was a pause on the other end. Then Daniel said, "I would be very concerned. First of all, I'd go to the person. I'd be very polite. I'd say, 'I'm concerned because I'm not convinced these results are real. How can you help me, what can we do, to make sure these results will hold up so we don't report something false?'"

"Suppose you already kind of tried that and it didn't work."

"I would tell the person I no longer wanted my name on the paper."

"Me neither," I said. "I don't want to be on the mosquito project with Alissa anymore."

"Hmm, that's a shame. Does that . . . does that mean you don't want me to proceed with the analysis?"

"Oh, no. I mean yes! I mean it's not that. I still want you to test my . . . what did you call them?"

"Emanations. Maybe you better tell me just what happened."

So I told him about Alissa's towel experiment.

"Very clever," Daniel said. "I like it."

"But you see, I don't think she really did it," I said miserably. "I mean, she wasn't gone long enough, and she wouldn't let me watch her, and she refused to repeat it or let other people try."

"Hm," said Daniel. "All bad signs. I think you're right, Nala. That's something you can't sign your name to."

"But do I tell the teacher?"

"Ah," he said. "That's a tough one. Whistle blowers often suffer. But you know, the teacher is going to ask why you pulled out."

"Kids don't tell on each other," I said. "That's something we don't do."

Daniel didn't seem to have an answer to that. Instead, he invited me back to the lab to see what he was doing with my smells. "I think it will make you feel better," he said.

I did go to the lab, and I did feel better, as if Daniel was my partner instead of Alissa.

On the morning the project was due, Alissa carried in her folded poster board and told me excitedly, "I took your advice. More data."

She asked for my part about malaria to paste in the one space she had left. I just shook my head and told her I didn't have it.

When it came time to make our presentation, Alissa presented "our" poster alone. She had a diagram about mosquitoes and a photo from Daniel's microscope. She had a graph comparing the number of bites she received on her first trip by the brook—40—to the numbers she got the next three times—3, 4, and 2. I was pretty sure she had never actually counted the bites the first time, or ever even made the last two trips. For one thing, she hadn't harvested any more of my sweat. She had a graph showing the number of people who get sick every year from mosquito-borne diseases, like dengue or Zika or encephalitis or malaria, and she had a photo of me with my arm stuck through the white cloth sleeve into Daniel's mosquito-biting box.

"Do you have anything to add, Nala?" Mrs. Garment asked. I shook my head. I had some notes on my bean experiment stuffed in my desk, but the truth is the stupid bean plant never really grew, and when I went to talk to Mrs. Garment about it, she told me working with a partner was a non-negotiable part of the project. Even I didn't really care about the bean plant.

Mrs. Garment asked me to come see her during lunch period.

"I don't understand," she said. "I can see by Alissa's photographs that you were very involved in the early part of this project. But then you slacked off. This has become something of a pattern with you, Nala. You start with enthusiasm and then you quit. You ask questions and then you zone out. Are you overtired? Are you having problems at home? Did you have a falling-out of some sort with Alissa? I know she can be domineering at times, but she has so much to offer." She sighed. "I do believe I'm going to have to call your mother again. I hate to burden her."

This is the way it is with Mrs. Garment. She sounds concerned at first, but she really can't be interested in what students have to say, because she piles on the questions too fast for a person to think of an answer. And then she jumps in with the zinger, guilt.

Only this time she pressed harder. "What is it?" she asked. "Why did you stop cooperating with Alissa? Did something about the project upset you?"

"It was the towel, and the sweat," I said.

"That made you squeamish?"

This was turning out all wrong. I didn't have any actual proof that Alissa had cheated. And I remembered what I'd told Daniel, that kids don't rat each other out. So I gave up.

I said, "Have you ever heard of Henrietta Lacks?"

eleven

On Saturday morning, just a day after Mrs. Garment called home about my D on the science project, the doorbell rang and my mom asked me to answer it. On the doorstep stood Daniel Wright, in jeans and without his embroidered lab coat. A Labrador retriever stood at his side.

"Your mother said it was all right to bring Harry," he said. "May we come in?"

I backed into the house, too surprised to reply. Harry the dog stepped up and thrust his nose into my crotch. Daniel pulled him back, but my face burned, as I thought about how even a dog was interested mostly in how I smelled.

I worried that maybe Daniel, who had talked to me on the phone almost as if I were a fellow scientist, had come to consult with my mom about my terrible science project and my erratic performance in school.

Instead, he sat on the couch, and Harry sat politely on the floor beside him.

"Nala, honey, will you make Daniel some of your delicious tea?" my mother asked.

While I was in the kitchen boiling water and crumbling fresh mint leaves, I heard the two of them talking softly in the living room. It was all a setup, I could tell. My mom was going to get me evaluated for ADD again, and she had brought in Daniel, as a scientist, to make the whole thing sound like a good idea.

I carried Daniel's cup in and set it on the table beside him hard enough to make it splash. He looked up at me, his eyes wide with surprise. "Bad week?" he asked.

"No kidding," I told him.

My mom said, "Nala's teachers can be short-sighted sometimes." And that was it. She didn't tell him about her phone call from Mrs. Garment the night before, or about our long conversation afterward, where my mom told me that life is a struggle, but a beautiful one, and we all have to rise above people who doubt us even as we work to overcome our own weaknesses.

"I've been talking to your mother about something that might cheer you up," Daniel said.

"I haven't said yes yet," my mother put in.

"What is it?" I asked. And then a crazy idea grabbed me. "My dad?"

Daniel shook his head. "It doesn't make sense to bring people here one at a time. I'm interested in whole family trees, in inheritance patterns."

"He wants an introduction to Robert's whole family," my mother said.

Daniel leaned forward. "Alissa showed me your project poster."

"Not mine," I said.

Daniel waved my comment away. "She showed her father too, and along with the data I've shared with him, that convinced him. He's announced that Drossila will fund an exploratory expedition to Kenya."

"To Kenya?" I repeated stupidly.

"Yes, to try and identify a whole family of people resistant to mosquito bites, and to test them for the chemicals in their skin so we can find the common ingredient."

"You're going to Kenya," I repeated. "You want me to put you in touch with my father."

"Oh, much more than that," Daniel said. "I want you to come along."

twelve

I looked back and forth between Daniel and my mom. My mother's hands gripped the armrests of her wheelchair hard enough to make her fingernail beds white. "Are we going to do it?" I asked her.

"You know I don't fly," she said. She let out a breath. "I'd like to take you, sweetie, I really would, but air travel is the one thing I don't have courage for. To wheel myself onto a plane—I know my arms would just freeze up."

I'll wheel you on, I wanted to tell her, but I could see that she was actually trembling. "So I can't go?" I burst out. I didn't mean it to come out sounding angry, but it did. Why bring Daniel here at all, if she was just going to keep me from going?

Mom gripped the wheelchair handles. "I'm still wrestling with it," she said. The way the muscles stood out in her forearms, she really did look like she was wrestling, maybe trying to twist her wheelchair's metal framework into some other shape. "One possibility is that Nick could go with you."

"That's right," Daniel said. "Mr. Bowen has authorized a travel spot for Nick." He scratched his head. "And because we know the prospect of a working safari with a couple of older men like us may feel a little awkward, we're also inviting a friend your own age."

Jolene, I thought wildly, and I jumped to my feet. *They're bringing Jolene.*

Daniel nodded, looking grave. "That's right. A key member of this trip will be Alissa."

So there it was. My superpower had won me the thing I wanted most in the world, a trip to Kenya to see my family. I should have been dancing in my seat all day every day at school. Instead I felt unsettled. I avoided Alissa, who was telling everybody about our trip, and how she had talked her father into it, and how Drossila was paying for everything, and how we were even going to go on safari and camp in a place where you could hear lions roar at night. But other than putting her arm over my shoulder as she told other people about our trip, she hardly spoke to me at all. "Aren't you going to apologize to her?" Elizabeth asked me.

"What for?" I asked.

"Whatever you did. Whatever she's mad at you about." Seeing me look blank, Elizabeth leaned close. "You don't even have to know what it is. Just apologize. She's very forgiving. And otherwise, you never know, she might change her mind about the trip."

I just shook my head.

I told Jolene about it at lunch. We were sitting at a picnic table outside for once. Jolene snorted. "Maybe Alissa wants you to suck up to her the way Elizabeth does, but her dad's the one giving you the trip. I think you'll be okay."

I peeled the foil top off my fruit cup, spilling a bit of the sugar water onto my skirt. "Maybe it would be a good thing if Alissa did change her mind."

"What's wrong with you?" Jolene asked. "You're going to Africa, girl. What are you moping around for? You scared of some raggedy old lions?"

I poked at my fruit cup. I hate the way the grapes in fruit cups are so pale and peeled, like blind eyeballs. "With Nick and me both gone, who's going to take care of my mother?"

"What do you mean? Your mom's a grownup."

"I sleep in her room at night. I help her get up to go to the bathroom."

"You do? You never told me that. No wonder you fall asleep so much at school." Jolene considered. "How does your mom manage all day when she's at work?"

"She takes herself to the bathroom. I mean, I know she can do it. It's harder to get up from bed, when it's dark and everything, but I actually know she can handle it. It's just she'll be so worried and lonely."

"So your grandma will come stay with her."

"That's what I'm afraid of." Grandma Ronnie would get my mother all worked up. She'd conjure up plane crashes, lion attacks, raging elephants. She'd hint that a good mother would do anything to steer her daughter away from such danger.

Jolene gave me a poke. "What are you feeling so guilty for?"

I didn't really understand the answer to that myself. "I guess just that I didn't earn it. I didn't even do my fair half of the science project. All I did was sit in a lab and have mosquitoes not bite me."

"So you got lucky this once. You think Henrietta Lacks would turn down an all-expenses-paid trip to Africa?"

"I wish you were the one coming with me," I said.

"No lie, girl, so do I. Tell you what, when you're all rich and famous, you're taking me back there. I want to see some flamingoes."

I imagined myself swooping low over a lake just as a giant flock of pink birds rose from its surface. "I'll bring you a pink feather," I promised.

At the time, I had no idea where that promise would lead me.

thirteen

*T*o convince myself that I really did deserve to go to Africa, I decided to learn all I could about malaria. The next time we had library period at school, I found a book on tropical diseases, and after gawking for a while and getting grossed out by a bunch of skin diseases, I read about malaria. It was really confusing. The malaria parasite goes through all sorts of different life stages, first inside the mosquito, then inside the person the mosquito bites. I drew pictures of the malaria life cycle, colored them in with colored pencils, and mouthed the names of the different parasite stages: spor-o-zo-ite, mer-o-zo-ite.

While I worked at a round table, I heard giggling at one of the library computers. Alissa was working the keyboard, and two or three of her crew leaned in to watch. I wondered what could be so funny about searching for books. If they were looking for a funny book, though, it was too late, because the bell rang and it was time to move on to math.

I didn't see Jolene after school, so I walked home along the brook path, making taunting faces at any insects I saw. They didn't pay any attention to me.

Just before dinner, Jolene called. "I've set off a huge commotion," she said.

"What did you do?"

"It's not what I did. You know I have library right after you? Well, you won't believe this, but somebody left a message on one of the computers. Right in big capital letters, in the place where you enter the title you're searching for."

"A message for you?"

"A message for the world. They wrote, 'BLACK LIVES DON'T MATTER.'"

The phrase hit me like a sock in the stomach. Almost half the kids in our school are African American. Someone was saying it didn't matter if we lived or died. "What did you do?"

"I screeched. I didn't even mean to. I showed the librarian and then I went to the office. They're sending an email out to all the parents, and they're going to talk about it at a special assembly tomorrow. They're taking it really seriously."

"Someone probably meant it as a joke," I said weakly. An uncomfortable picture nibbled at my memory: Alissa and her friends, giggling.

"They meant it as a message," Jolene said. "They left it up on purpose for the next person to see. It's intimidation, harassment, cyber bullying. Did you see anything?"

"No," I lied.

"Well, try to remember. It was the computer second from the left when you face the window. They're going to be interviewing kids from your period."

I imagined teachers leaning in over me, shining a light in my face and asking questions while I shrank in my chair. "Jolene," I pleaded, "don't you think maybe we should let it go?"

Jolene gave a snort of disgust. "I can't believe you. Sometimes you sound like you're all white. Plain old white vanilla. Maybe that's just what you want to be."

"That's not true!"

"You can't turn white by refusing to stand with your own people, you know. Talk to your mom about it. She'll tell you this is important. And tomorrow I want you to stand by me when I talk about it. We have to make people see." Jolene hung up.

I didn't feel like eating dinner. My stomach acted like a washing machine that turns and stops, turns and stops, while soapy water sloshes around. Alissa wouldn't tolerate a tattle-tale. If I said anything, my trip to Africa would be gone for sure.

"Come sit with me," my mom said, after Nick and I finished the dishes. "Tell me what's bothering you."

I settled on the couch and clutched a cushion to my chest. "There was this thing that happened at school today."

"I just got an email about it."

I let the cushion drop to my lap. "So . . . the thing is, do you think it's such a big deal?"

"What do you mean?"

"Enough to get the whole school worked up? To divide the back kids from the white kids and make them face off?"

"Is that what you think is going to happen?" My mom peered at me. "You really must feel caught in the middle sometimes."

I shook my head. "I know I'm black."

She sighed. "Here in America you are. Back in Kenya, you'd be considered white. But to answer your question, yes, I think it's a big deal. Sure, someone probably thought they were being funny, but there was a lot of hostility there. Some student with a lot of privilege has just decided to strut that privilege around by putting other people down."

"So you'd say this person is a bad person?"

My mother shook her head. "Most people want to be good. Sometimes they just need a little help getting there, and the help can be tough. Whoever did this has a whole lot to learn, and they'd best learn it now while they're young."

I squeezed the cushion to my chest again. Finally, I said in a small voice, "But should a person ever tell on another student?"

My mother didn't answer for a while. She just watched me. I think she was waiting for me to find the answer on my own, but my mind just shut down and refused to think. Finally she said, "Two things. One, school is for learning. Two, and you know this: black lives do matter."

I meant to go to school early and talk to the principal. I really did, but I overslept, and I actually got to school just as the bell rang, so if I'd gone to the principal's office everyone would have seen me. We had the assembly, and the administration asked any students who were involved to come forward, and anyone who had any information to share it. Then Jolene stood up and asked for anyone who felt personally hurt or threatened to stand up, and we did, including a bunch of Hispanic and white students, which confused me. Then the principal asked anyone who objected to the message to stand with us, and everybody in the whole auditorium stood. Looking around at all the faces gave me a shivery feeling, and I thought maybe it didn't matter who wrote the message.

So that was that. The day went forward, and there was a lot of buzz among the students, but no real information. At lunch I sat uncomfortably down at one end of a table where Alissa was holding court, looking through early copies of the yearbook. Jolene sat with a group of activist students on the other side of the cafeteria.

Then, on the way into math class, the last class of the day, Tom Vledecky sidled up to me. "Do you hear what people are saying?" he asked. "They're saying Jolene wrote the message herself, to create a stir and get attention."

"That's crazy!"

"They're asking what's the chance that the angriest kid in school was the one to find that message?"

"Is that what you think?" I demanded. "You think Jolene did it just to get attention?"

Tom shrugged and looked down at his feet. "She *is* super political," he said.

I stopped short and hugged my books to my chest. "Um, I forgot something," I said. "You go on in. There's someplace I have to go."

That was it. Nobody was going to make up lies about Jolene and get away with it. I walked to the office, my footsteps sounding loud and determined in the empty corridor.

🦟 fourteen

Rumors swirled around the school. Alissa and two of her friends were suspended for three days, just as finals were about to start. Tom sat beside me at lunch and said, "That was really brave of you."

"What are you talking about?" I snapped at him, but he just offered to help me catch up on the math I had missed the day before.

As for Jolene, she never said anything about it to me directly, but she walked me home that first day of the girls' suspension, arm in arm and way out of her way, without even pausing by the soccer field.

When the three girls returned, two of them kept their eyes down and stayed away from Alissa as if their parents had really told them off, but Alissa seemed as cheerful and important as ever. "Of course I didn't deny anything," she told her table at lunchtime. "They didn't even listen to me. I was looking up an article I'd heard about. I was planning to write an editorial about it for the *Flag*."

The *Flag* is our school newspaper. For moment I wondered if Alissa could be telling the truth, but then Tom spoke up. "Funny, because the *Flag* has published its last issue for the year."

Alissa didn't blink. "Is there something wrong with preparing early for next year?" Anyway, it turned out wonderfully, she said, because her mom took her to see some shows in New York City while the rest of us were sweating through reviewing for finals. "My mom says the school's reaction was hysterical and stupid," Alissa said. "Next year my parents are going to send me to private school." She glared around the table at all of us. "At last."

Alissa didn't single me out, so I guess she didn't know I was the one who told the principal. Still, it was pretty hard to imagine us getting all close and friendly during our trip to Kenya.

Two days before the end of school, Daniel came over with his dog. It was after dinner, and my mother served him a brownie on a small plate. I brought out my brand new passport so I could show Daniel the picture wasn't too bad.

When he saw the passport, Daniel leaned down and fiddled with Harry's collar. "Did Alissa speak to you?" he asked.

I said no.

He looked up. "It seems her mother found her a special opportunity for the summer, modeling for a clothing company."

"Really?"

"It's a sort of training program. You know Alissa's parents are divorced?"

I didn't know.

My mom said, "Sometimes divorced parents end up vying for their children's affection."

"Buying?" I asked.

"Vying. Competing. Alissa is an only child."

I imagined Alissa's parents surrounding her with dresses and vacations and jewelry, pulling her this way and that, and I looked down at my own shorts, which were getting tight across the hips. *I could use some vying in my life*, I thought. I was shabby, and by fall, after her modeling gig, Alissa would be more fashionable and beautiful than ever. Of course, she wouldn't even be at the Elion School anymore, so people wouldn't notice the contrast between her and me. I made an effort not to envy her. "I don't really care what she does with the rest of her summer," I said.

"That's the problem." Daniel set his brownie plate on the arm of the couch and leaned forward, resting his elbows on his knees. "It's not about the rest of the summer. The modeling program is all summer long. Alissa has chosen it in place of the trip to Kenya."

"You mean the trip's off?" My voice rose high.

Daniel spread his hands. "Not the whole trip. Just the part where we bring you and Alissa and Nick."

"No fair!" I stamped my foot. I should have known something would fall through. This felt more than anything like Alissa's revenge on me. I folded my arms to hold in the surge of anger threatening to burst out of me.

Daniel steadied his plate of half-eaten brownie. "I probably shouldn't say this, but her father's pretty annoyed with her."

"Annoyed!" my mother said. "He should be furious. To throw the chance of a lifetime back in his face this way."

I wondered if Mr. Bowen had told Alissa off for leaving that racist message on the library computer, and then her mother had comforted her with the trip to New York City, and then mother and daughter had cooked up this summer experience as a way to show her mean old father that they didn't care what he thought. I practically shouted, "So, fine, then. We go without her. We never needed her anyway. I'm the one who's supposed to introduce you to my relatives. I'm the one mosquitoes won't bite. Who cares about Alissa?"

Daniel stood, and to my surprise, he smiled. "I hoped that was what you would say. I want you to come to Kenya with us. Now I just have to talk to Mr. Bowen and convince him that you're my indispensable assistant."

I wanted to say, *Tell him to teach his spoiled daughter a lesson!* but it didn't really seem like a good idea.

My mother folded her hands and nodded. "That's the way, Nala," she said. "Stand up for yourself."

Stand up for yourself. Put your best foot forward. Just take the first step. Have you noticed how many motivational phrases assume a person can walk? But my mom was really supporting me. With that, the last of my ambivalence melted away. My mother wanted me to go on this trip, just like Jolene did, unselfishly.

Jolene. I decided to push my luck. "Ask if I can bring Jolene instead," I suggested.

The next day at school, Alissa confronted me. Her gloss-covered lips twisted into a smirk. "I guess you heard the trip's off."

My heart thumped, but then I figured out that Daniel hadn't had his chance yet to persuade her father. I crossed my fingers. "Actually, I didn't," I said, and I spun away and left her there.

I didn't say anything to Jolene, and I guess that was good, because that evening Daniel called. "We're on, but it's a work trip only," he said. "No safari, and no Jolene. Mr. Bowen doesn't want the company taking responsibility for another young girl."

I felt bad about Jolene, but waves of excitement swept through me. "Is Nick still coming?" I asked.

"Nick's coming along to help with the work," Daniel said. "And he can lurk around Mr. Bowen and learn the secrets to getting rich."

"Mr. Bowen's coming?" I asked. Then I lowered my voice and said apologetically. "One thing about Nick. Even if it's going to be a great educational experience, you know he likes to get paid."

Daniel laughed. "He's getting paid all right. And although we can't fully pay you, because child labor is illegal, the company plans to donate to your college fund."

MOSQUITOES DON'T BITE ME

I danced around, holding the phone and chanting silently, "Yes, yes, yes!"

During the last two days of school, girls gathered around Alissa as she paged through spreads from fashion magazines and bragged about her mother's connections with modeling agencies in New York. When I passed by, she narrowed her eyes and shook her head in pity at my lack of fashion. In return I sent her my most dazzling smile. We didn't speak.

fifteen

On June twelfth, Mom drove Nick and me to the airport to see us off. She didn't want to come in, so she just dropped us at the curb, acting casual, as if she drove to the airport all the time. She kissed me goodbye and gave a little wave. "Stay away from al-Shabaab," she told Nick, and to me she said, "Give my love to your father."

Her love? Were people supposed to divorce if they loved each other? As she drove away, I asked Nick, "What's al-Shabaab?"

"Islamic terrorists from Somalia. They like to come over the border to blow people up or kidnap them. Don't worry, we're not going anywhere near that part of the country. That's just your mom being nervous." Nick lifted both our bags. "Come on. It's going to take us an hour to lug this bag of yours up to the counter."

Actually, my duffle ended up not much bigger than Nick's, though I have to admit I had some trouble deciding what to pack. Lots of books and a journal, but those went in my backpack for the plane ride. Photos of Mom and Jolene. A jar of peanut butter because someone told me they don't have that in foreign countries. Baseball caps to give my cousins. My mom insisted I could only bring one stuffed animal, which made for a hard choice. Dolphin, owl, panda? I decided I should bring one of the African animals to see its native land. In the end I chose Hannibal the baby elephant.

Jeans, shorts, skirts, sandals, sneakers, nice shoes, one of those photographer's vests with lots of pockets, a sun hat, sunglasses, sunscreen. Even mosquito repellant. My mom insisted. "The mosquitoes are different out there," she said. "You never know."

Now that was a sobering thought. What if we got to Kenya and it turned out that Anopheles mosquitoes, the kind that spread malaria, actually liked the way I smelled? Mr. Bowen would blow his top and load us right onto the next plane home.

Flying to Africa takes approximately forever. First we flew to New York, then to Amsterdam in the Netherlands, and finally to Nairobi, which is the capital city of Kenya. I sat in a row three across with Uncle Nick and Daniel, and they let me have the window seat for every takeoff and landing. It was my first time on a plane since I was three years old, and I kept my face close to the window, watching the cars and buildings and streets shrink away below me, and then breathing deeply as we passed through the clouds. I wanted to jump right out the window and bounce on the fluffy white billows, even though I know they're only tiny water droplets and I would fall right through. I suppose everyone feels that same way the first time they fly over clouds.

Then I imagined the clouds opening and revealing Kenya below me, green and five-sided the way it showed up on our globe at home. I would slip through my fluffy cloud and float down, maybe with a parachute just to be sure, watching as the map enlarged into actual cities and lakes and mountains and sweeping grassland.

I bounced around my seat, too fidgety to read or draw, until Nick told me to settle down and watch a movie. Then I tried to calm down so Daniel wouldn't get tired of me.

About an hour after we left New York, Mr. Bowen came back to check on us. It was my first time meeting him. He was shorter than I expected, and he was balding on top, but he looked fit and relaxed, wearing a blue blazer and khaki pants and a pink polo shirt. "Everybody cozy and comfortable back here?" he asked.

"Where is he sitting?" I asked Daniel after he left.

"First class," Daniel said. "Upstairs."

"They have an upstairs?" I asked, amazed. So that was that bulge I'd noticed on top of the plane. "I'd like to see that."

Nick said, "That's not for the *hoi-polloi* like us. *Hoi-polloi*, the common people, the worker bees." He looked kind of cross, so I decided not to remind him worker bees are all female.

Daniel said, "I'm just grateful for the chance to do our research, and in such fine company as the two of you." He shifted his legs around, trying to get them to fit better in the cramped space.

"So how's it going to work?" Nick asked. "What do you think is going on with Nala's family?"

"That's the question," Daniel said. He fingered his little King Tut beard. "It's intriguing. We think mosquitoes have been carrying malaria in Africa for tens of thousands of years, so we might expect people to have evolved different ways of resisting it."

He explained that malaria is a parasite, a single-celled organism that enters a person's red blood cells and multiplies there. Eventually the red cell bursts and the person gets anemia. And sometimes capillaries, which are tiny blood vessels, get clogged with misshapen blood cells and parasites. "When that happens, tissue dies," he said. "If it happens in the kidneys, your urine turns dark and your kidneys start to get destroyed. If it happens in the brain, you can get seizures or even die. Meanwhile, along comes another mosquito and sucks up some of your blood, picking up lots of parasites along the way. And then the parasites, which are called Plasmodium, go to the mosquito's gut and then move into her salivary glands, all ready to be injected into the next person she bites."

I shivered. "You didn't mention the sporozoites and merozoites." I wanted Daniel to think I was smart.

"How do people resist it?" Nick asked.

"Some people's red blood cells make it hard for the Plasmodium parasite to enter."

"People can change their red blood cells?" I asked, incredulous.

"Not on purpose. Some people are born with a difference in their red blood cells that changes their shape. Have you heard of sickle cell anemia?"

I nodded, thinking of Freddie Dixon in fourth grade. "You get swollen joints and fever and have to go to the hospital."

"That's right. People with sickle cell have red blood cells that change shape when they aren't carrying much oxygen. They get bent and stiff, like little crescent moons instead of nice blobby spheres. Some of the blood cells get chewed up, and some get stuck in capillaries."

"And that causes the swelling and pain?"

"Yes, every once in a while. It's called a sickle cell crisis, and people need to be treated for the pain. They also have trouble with certain kinds of infection. The only good part is that the red blood cells in sickle cell anemia don't get infected with the malaria parasite."

"Oh, great," I said. "Instead of malaria, you get to go the hospital all the time for terrible pain."

"You're right, it's not a great tradeoff," Daniel said. "But here's the thing. To have sickle cell anemia, you have to get two copies of DNA with the same change in them, one from your mother and one from your father. If you only get one copy of changed DNA, from one parent, it's called sickle cell trait, and you don't have real sickle cells, but your red blood cells are still resistant to malaria."

"You mean you don't get anemia and you don't get malaria?"

"Exactly. Best of both worlds. So you see why the trait persists in the population."

"Huh?" I said. Although I wanted Daniel to think I was smart, he was confusing me.

"For thousands of years, people who happened to be born with sickle cell trait were protected from malaria. They were more likely to survive childhood, to grow up and have children of their own. But there was a catch. If the other parent had sickle cell trait too, one-fourth of their children would be born with sickle cell anemia, and without modern medicine, that child would probably never survive to have children. Sickle cell trait was both a blessing and a curse."

I thought about that for a while. "The blessing part only matters in places with malaria. In America, it's no advantage to have sickle cell trait."

"That's a very astute observation," Daniel said. "We think that's why we only find sickle cell trait and sickle cell anemia in people of African descent. For people whose ancestors have always lived in places without malaria, the trait, if it arose by mistake, would just tend to die out."

Nick leaned in from the aisle. "Okay, so some African people evolved a way for their red blood cells to resist infection, but it kind of stank, because some of their children would die. Why not just evolve a way to resist the mosquitoes in the first place?"

"And that is exactly why Nala is so interesting," Daniel said. "Somewhere, one of her ancestors probably had a little change in their DNA that made a skin compound that was slightly different, and, just by chance, it drove mosquitoes away. Well, think about it. Anybody with a trait like that should have a big survival advantage. No malaria! You'd expect that person to pass the trait on to half their offspring, and you'd expect it to spread. So I'm hoping we'll find the trait in lots of Nala's relatives."

"Unless Nala's the first mutant," Nick said helpfully.

Daniel shot me a look. "Let's not say *mutant*," he suggested. "How about *highly evolved being*? But Nala's father says her family is too strong to get malaria, so I think that's a very good sign that we'll find some others."

I sat there, feeling a little glow all over my skin because I was a highly evolved being. But then Nick said, "I wonder if there's a downside, like with sickle cell? I mean, don't you think Nature always finds a balance? What if Nala gets some mysterious sickness later in life?"

"Nonsense," Daniel said. He looked really annoyed, and he patted me on the knee and then quickly withdrew his hand as if he'd been improper.

I'm a mutant, I thought. *Maybe that's why I have trouble paying attention in school.*

sixteen

Nick carried my duffel along with his own out of customs into the main chamber of the Nairobi airport. I could hardly keep my feet from skipping and dancing, I was so excited. I cast my glance around and immediately caught sight of my father, taller than everyone else, with his straight black eyebrows and his hair shorter than I remembered from our last Skype call, holding a sign that said *KARIBU, NALA!* as if he was afraid maybe I wouldn't recognize him.

"*Karibu* means welcome in Swahili," Mr. Bowen said, turning his head to the side, as if he was telling the world in general. He probably thought I didn't know.

My father lowered his sign and came to meet us at the end of the barrier. He threw his arms around me and lifted me off the floor, backpack and all. Then he pumped the hands of Nick, Mr. Bowen, and Daniel. In person, my father was the blackest person I have ever seen, darker even than Jolene, much darker than Daniel. "I am Robert Simiyu," he told the men. "And this is my wife Alice."

My mouth fell open and I stumbled back a step. His wife! Standing beside him, she was a foot shorter, smiling, pretty, full of curves. She wore a green print dress, and she had dimples. She reached for me and pulled me into a hug, but against her softness my body felt like a frozen slab of meat. "Nobody told me you were married," I said past her shoulder to my father.

Alice let me go. "I have told him and told him not to surprise you," she said. "Men are cowards. They are afraid to say things."

My father turned his hands upward. "I wanted you to meet Alice first," he said. "I knew when you met her you would love her."

"Does Mom know?" I asked, accusingly.

"Of course, of course. It has been many years."

The six of us stood in an awkward circle for a moment. Nick's mouth hung open, telling me my father's marriage was news to him also. Mr. Bowen's toe tapped as if he didn't understand the fuss and was in a hurry to get going. Daniel put an arm around me and gave me a quick squeeze.

"Let's move along," Mr. Bowen said. "What's the plan here?"

Daniel spoke up. "Nala will go home to rest at her father's house while the rest of us check into the hotel. Then we meet up for supper at—where is it?"

"The Carnivore," my father said. "African game meat, all you can eat."

Traffic clogged the streets of Nairobi. Alice sat in the back so I could have the front passenger seat, but I didn't talk to my father. I sat with my face pressed against the window, watching the people walk along the sidewalks or hold up toys or fruit for sale. My stomach hurt. I couldn't believe my parents had kept this little detail from me. I felt as if my father had kicked over a huge pot of hope inside of me and now the hope was spilling out onto the dry ground. *I thought they might get back together,* I realized. *My mother said to give him her love. I thought he might come home with me.*

"I feel sick," I said.

My father told me to roll down the window and stick my face out in the breeze. The air was mild, no warmer than at home, but it smelled of exhaust and smoky food. We hit a traffic jam, and a swarm of skinny men and boys wound their way among the vehicles, selling bananas, paper cones of peanuts, flashlights, candy, and cheap plastic toys. One boy thrust a half-burnt cob of corn at me, and then, catching sight of my face, pointed at me in delight, calling out, "Mzungu! Mzungu!"

I drew back. "What is he calling me?"

Alice spoke from the back seat. "He says, 'White person! See the white person!'"

I rolled up my window, leaving the smell of corn behind, but soon another boy pressed a stuffed giraffe against the window and gestured emphatically with his other hand. Even when the traffic started up again, the boy ran alongside us, wiggling his giraffe until we sped away from him.

Alice reached forward to rub my neck. I shrugged her soft hands off of me.

It turned out I had five little half-brothers and sisters: Adam, Mary, Susie, Jacob and Benjamin. Adam, who looked about ten, hung back, glowering at me, obviously feeling the same way I felt about him, but the little ones crowded around me. "You said they were my cousins," I told my father over their heads. I blinked to dam my tears.

"Cousins and siblings, they are very similar in our culture," my father said.

Alice rolled her eyes. "What nonsense you talk, Robert. Now children, we should let Nala wash up and rest. Adam, please bring Nala's bag."

Adam swung my duffel through a door and set it on the ground. Mary and Jacob took my hands and led me through the door into a tiny bedroom with a freshly made bed. A light cotton bedspread printed with purple elephants against a golden background covered the bed, and a towel and washcloth lay at its foot. Above the bed a mosquito net with thin mesh hung suspended.

Mary showed me the way to the bathroom. Then their mother called the children away, and I flung myself on the bed and wept.

"We must play the hand we are dealt, Nala," my mother says, although she doesn't play cards. After a while, the hollow feeling in my stomach began to feel like hunger. I got up from the bed, turned over the pillow so the wet spot didn't show, and went to the bathroom to take a shower. The water trickled and sputtered, turning hot and cold. I put on a dress and sandals and came out into the main room.

Benjamin sat on the floor in his diaper, pushing a toy truck around. Adam was out somewhere. Susie and Mary sat on a drooping couch looking at magazines together and giggling. Jacob turned to his mother and asked, "Can I bang now?" He grabbed a pot and a spoon and marched around the room clanging the pot with his spoon. "He wanted to have a parade for you," Alice said apologetically.

"Where's my father?" I asked.

"He had to finish one thing at work," Alice said, and then she pointed to the computer. "He thought you might want to Skype your mother."

The computer booted up slowly.

"Now, Jacob," Alice said, "this is the silent part of the parade where you just wave your arms and dance."

With Jacob waving his arms and dancing, I reached my mother. When she came on, I forgot to tell her I had a good flight and arrived safely. "You should have told me," I said.

"Honey, I wanted to. Your father always said he had to be the one to tell you himself."

"But obviously he didn't," I said. Adults can be so stupid sometimes.

My mom and I didn't have too much to say after that. I was relieved when a library patron came up behind her and asked where to find a book of Moroccan recipes.

Alice and the children didn't come to dinner at the Carnivore. My father drove me there, and he tried to point things out along the way. We passed an airport in a broad, flat field. "This is the Wilson Airport," he said. "The Flying Doctors flew from here."

"Do you still fly?" I asked.

His smile seemed a little sad. "Sometimes, when I have to go inspect the roads. But nowadays I let someone else fly the plane."

My father, Alice had told me with pride, was Deputy Minister of Transportation for the newly elected government. But he didn't even fly anymore, he looked at roads. It was the most boring thing I could think of. After that I just stared out the side window, not looking where my father pointed. I figured it was no use acting all interested. A man with five children at home might go through the motions, but he is not going to waste a lot of affection on a foreign daughter from a forgotten first wife.

Before we got out of the car at the Carnivore, my father handed me a white cell phone. "This is a prepaid phone, Nala, because your American phone won't work here. See, I've put my number on speed dial, so all the time you're in Kenya I can be right beside you in a minute if you ever need me."

Inside the restaurant we sat at long tables under hanging globes of light while waiters came around bearing huge skewers of meat. If you wanted something, they pulled out their long knives and sawed off a slice. Antelope meat, beef, giraffe, warthog, crocodile.

"I hear crocodile tastes like chicken," Nick said, and he added it to the big pile of meat on his plate like some greedy hyena. I tried a tiny bite of antelope because I thought it might be tender, but then I thought of the living antelope leaping through the grass and I just felt sick to my stomach again.

"I have brought you a list of my family," my father told Daniel. He unfolded a sheaf of papers and handed them across the table. "Ninety-three relatives, mostly still living in the village."

Daniel examined the list. "This is very helpful, Mr. Simiyu."

"Please, call me Robert."

Mr. Bowen spoke up. "Tomorrow, Robert, we would like to show you the new lab Drossila is sponsoring at the university. As you may know, we are hoping to build the expertise of native Kenyans to the point where we can create a drug manufacturing facility here."

"We appreciate it, Mr. Bowen," my father said. "Our government is disposed to help in any way we can to build new industry in Kenya."

Mr. Bowen nodded with a small smile, but I noticed he did not invite my father to call him by his first name.

A waiter came and, slicing from a haunch of eland, which is a big old antelope with spiral horns, spoke into my father's ear. I only heard because I sat next to my father and leaned close. The waiter said, "Did you hear, Minister? Al-Shabaab has attacked the coast again, near Mombasa. A pair of German tourists has been snatched away."

My father raised his hand and said, "Not here, Thomas, not now."

The waiter dipped his head and backed away.

My mostly empty stomach flip-flopped. Al-Shabaab kidnappers, and my father not sharing news that might upset someone. I wondered how far it was to Mombasa, and whether kidnappers would want to snatch an American girl like me.

seventeen

I slept poorly, partly because of jet lag, but partly because bitter thoughts picked at my mind. I felt as though I had turned to read an old familiar book, the story of my life, and found the pages torn and smudged. My story used to have certain chapters: my parents' love story, the tragic accident, a separation between two people who still loved each other. Far apart, my two parents struggled on in their separate lives, and I was their daughter, their little lioness, bravely carrying on with an injured mother and a distant father. I wasn't like other kids who had divorced parents or absent fathers: my family was still bound close by love, even if separated by distance.

But it turned out my father just went out and got himself a new family, leaving my mother and me stranded and alone. I hated him. Hated his tall elegance, the way the waiter Thomas deferred to him, his friendly wife, his rollicking children. I wanted to go home.

I woke with a headache. The kids were thumping around in the next room, and I smelled something frying. Angry as I was, I was also starving, so I dressed in black slacks and a sleeveless, peach-colored blouse. "Very professional-looking," my mother had said. I wanted to look professional for our trip to the university.

All the kids had eaten already, and my father was away at the office again, but Alice served me sausage and fruit and boiled eggs and milky tea. There was some regular porridge, and beside it a bowl of an odd, pale yellow substance that also looked like porridge. "This is ugali," she said. "It's made from maize meal, corn meal. Some people eat it three times a day." Alice sat down across from me. *Stepmother*, I thought, trying out the word in my mind.

"Soon Robert will come pick you up to bring you to the university," Alice said. "He invited Adam to come too, but the naughty boy shook his head and ran away."

I wished I could run away like Adam.

Alice sat with her hands in her lap, watching me eat. "Robert says you started this whole mosquito project by yourself. He is so proud of you. Your father thinks you may be a famous scientist someday."

My spoonful of porridge caught in my throat. I hadn't told my father about my D on the science project. Maybe this thing of not sharing upsetting news went both ways.

I managed to swallow, and asked, "Have you ever had malaria?"

"Many times, with a nasty headache and a fever. When we have malaria, we rush to the clinic, where the doctor takes a smear of blood and looks at it under the microscope, and then gives us medicine. If you catch it early and get the right medicine, malaria is not so bad." She considered for a moment. "Adam has had malaria, and so has Mary, but not the other children."

When I didn't answer, she went on, "There are not very many mosquitoes here in Nairobi, and we always sleep under mosquito nets, so I am not certain if mosquitoes are eager to bite my other three children or if they just want to fly the other way."

"If malaria can be treated so easily, why do people die?"

"Sometimes it's a long way to the clinic, or people can't afford to go. Some medicines don't work on our malaria anymore, and the medicine that does work can be expensive. Some people go to native healers instead, but that may be a bad idea. The ones most likely to die are children, and especially babies." Saying this, Alice stood and swept up baby Benjamin, who had been crawling on the floor putting toys in his mouth.

I rode with my father to the university in an official ministry car with an actual chauffeur. Mr. Bowen arrived a few minutes later, and even though we had all introduced ourselves he introduced us again, Nick, Daniel, my father and me to a middle-aged professor named Matthew Munyole. Professor Munyole took us to a lab on the third floor. I felt as if I recognized it: lab benches, hoods, the rooms off to the side where the mosquitoes would be kept. How strange that it looked so much like the lab at home. I had an odd feeling of comfort, as if labs everywhere might be connected in some way, and even as if I might belong in one. It seemed that every lab station had a university student in a white coat working on something under the microscope.

"They are dissecting mosquitoes," Professor Munyole told us. "They are learning to identify which are the males and which are the females."

"Is that so you can tell the males and females apart," I asked, "because only the females drink blood?"

The professor ignored my question. "Under the microscope, it is not so difficult to tell the sexes apart. Males have much more feathery antennae, and the end of their abdomen is divided into two claspers to hold the female. Now we are looking inside the male mosquito at the testes. We are working on a project to make male mosquitoes sterile, so when a male mates with a female she does not succeed in laying eggs. Have you heard of this approach?"

I shook my head.

"The program is to release large numbers of sterile males in an area to occupy all the females and cut the number of mosquitoes way down in the next generation. But we want to be able to sort and identify male and female mosquitoes."

In the side room, stacks of mosquito boxes stood on shelves along one wall. Professor Munyole lifted one down.

"Anopheles?" Daniel asked. I knew that was the name of the mosquito that carries malaria. It's pronounced "Un-OFF-uh-lees."

"Yes, but don't worry, these mosquitoes are not infected with malaria or anything else," the professor said. "Who wants to try being bitten?"

"I will," I said. This was a little ritual I went through, I thought, in each new laboratory. It was like my ticket, the thing that made them all take me seriously, the most important thing about me. I put my arm through the sleeve and my hand into the box. I worried that Anopheles mosquitoes might have more refined taste and like the smell of me, but none landed on my skin. After a while, nodding in satisfaction, the professor told me I had passed the test.

My father went next. He unbuttoned his cuff and rolled up the sleeve of his tailored shirt, and with a grimace he plunged his hand into the mosquito box. He was like me: no mosquitoes landed. Daniel let out a low, happy whistle.

Nobody really wanted to go next. Finally, Daniel stepped up. As soon as his hand entered the box, the wispy mosquitoes dove in to attack him. Professor Munyole said, "Pull out, Dr. Wright. No need for fruitless suffering." Then he turned to Mr. Bowen. "You, sir?"

Mr. Bowen backed away. "I'm not part of the investigation."

I thought I saw a curve of amusement touch the professor's lips, and it occurred to me that even if Mr. Bowen was funding his research, the two men didn't like each other much.

When we left the mosquito room, Mr. Bowen said to Professor Munyole, "We should discuss your equipment needs. You have no HPLC machine, no scent extractor, is that right?"

"These are things we need," Professor Munyole agreed. "We have applied for a government grant to provide them."

Mr. Bowen clapped him on the back. "And how long will that take? I hear your new president is no big believer in science. Drossila will be happy to provide the equipment you need."

"Very generous," Professor Munyole said. But there was something in his tone that did not sound delighted.

"Let's pull aside and discuss some terms," Mr. Bowen said. "We don't need to drag our feet. We want to go upcountry as soon as the day after tomorrow. Minister Simiyu has kindly arranged a conclave of members of his extended family, so we need to update our research agreement."

The professor led Mr. Bowen toward another side room, and both Daniel and my father followed. I decided I didn't need to. Instead I approached one of the students and asked, "Will you show me what you see in the microscope?"

The young woman raised her head and regarded me through large round glasses. "Are you the one from America?" she asked.

I knew what she was really asking. "Yes. Mosquitoes don't bite me." As an afterthought, I added, "My name is Nala."

"And I am Ruth," she said, shaking my hand. She nodded with her lips pressed together, looking impressed. Then she showed me how to adjust the microscope dials, and together we made a drawing of the mosquito's body parts and decided it was a female. As we finished, the men emerged from the conference room.

"There you are," my father said to me. "For a moment I worried you disappeared."

"It seems one of my students kidnapped her," Professor Munyole said.

Ruth spoke up for me. "She helped me complete my assignment. When I am a medical doctor, I will remember the assistance given me by Nala."

"You're going to be a doctor!" I said, surprised and somehow proud of her.

"As a child I was like you, soaking up knowledge every chance I found," Ruth said.

That doesn't sound like me at all, I thought. I wondered if everyone in Kenya was so kind and optimistic, or whether maybe she was just sucking up to the professor or my father. But when we left the laboratory, Ruth gave me a quick hug and said, "Thank you for what you are doing for us." I felt more confused than ever as we rode down the elevator.

eighteen

The following morning, which was Saturday, my father took the family to the Giraffe Center in Nairobi. Daniel and Nick came too, but they rode behind us in a taxi with my two oldest stepsiblings, Adam and Mary. The three littler kids crawled all over me in the back seat. I was the only one wearing a seatbelt. We drove past what seemed like a whole city of tiny shacks with wavy tin roofs and winding, puddled tracks between them. Wires draped haphazardly between the roofs of some of the shacks. Children played in the puddles between the huts, poking at the mud with sticks. Their heads looked big compared to their bodies.

My father shook his head. "No proper roads, no plumbing, no electricity. These are squatters, Nala. They steal electricity when they can, but it's dangerous."

I looked back as we drove smoothly past on the newly paved highway. "Why doesn't the government fix it up?"

"Money," my father said. "Always money."

At the giraffe center, we climbed a stairway to a wooden platform, and the giraffes approached us for food. They walked with a dipping gait, swaying forward and back. Their front legs were much longer than their back ones, and they had short tails that they twitched back and forth. We bought pellets of pressed hay and grain, and Adam was the first to hold out the pellets in his flattened palm. An elegant giraffe approached and stuck out a long, black tongue.

"Put some food on the tongue," my father said.

Adam did so, and the great black tongue curled and swept the pellets back into the giraffe's mouth.

The rest of us clamored around my father for a chance to try. Only Susie hung back, saying, "I don't like that tongue!"

"But it is such a fine, strong tongue," my father said. "A giraffe will wrap his tongue around branches of the thorny acacia tree and strip its leaves without getting hurt."

Susie shuddered, but I held my arm outstretched as a young giraffe approached me. My hand shook a little. The pattern of brown polygons rippled on the giraffe's neck, and his brown eyes regarded me with solemn trust. His head reached just about the height of my hand. He stretched his head toward me, and then his surprising black tongue snaked out of his mouth. Carefully, I dropped giraffe pellets on the alien tongue and gazed into the giraffe's eyes as it rolled the tongue back into its mouth. *We are both Kenyan*, I told the giraffe silently. *We are family.*

After the giraffes, we returned to the university. This time the lab was mostly empty, except for Professor Munyole, who led us into the mosquito room. Alice was the first to put her arm through the sleeve. She squeezed her eyes tight shut as the mosquitoes landed and bit. After that, the kids took their turns one by one. Adam glared at me in a fury as the mosquitoes attacked his hand. They also bit Mary, but not Susie or Jacob. When it was Benjamin's turn, he wriggled as Alice tried to stuff his arm through the cotton sleeve leading into the mosquito box. Because the sleeve was longer than his arm, she had to pull it up around his arm up to his shoulder. He cried as the mosquitoes attacked him.

Professor Munyole showed the family around the rest of the lab, letting the middle kids look through microscopes and turning on the hood fans so they could hear the whooshing sound. Daniel found a sheet of paper and showed me how to make a family tree that indicated whether a genetic trait was present or absent. He made a square and colored it in with blue ink. "Here is your father, and he has the trait of repelling mosquitoes." He drew a horizontal line on each side of my father and made open circles. "Here are his two wives, and neither one of them repels mosquitoes, so we don't color them in." From the lines connecting my father to my mother, he dropped a vertical line and showed me as a colored-in circle. Then he dropped another line down from the line between my father and Alice. "Now you can fill in your brothers and sisters," Daniel said.

"You mean my *half*-brothers and sisters," I said. When Daniel didn't react to that, I made two open squares for Adam and Benjamin, an open circle for Mary, a colored-in circle for Susie, and a colored-in square for Jacob. It was funny. Coloring in the shapes made me feel like I was protecting them from malaria, and I wished I could color the other shapes too.

"Perfect," Daniel said. "A family chart like this is what we call a *pedigree*. And now when we go to Kitale tomorrow, we'll bring a lot more sheets of paper, for your father's siblings and cousins and nieces and nephews. First we'll ask them if they've ever had malaria. We'll check their temperature to make sure they're not sick now. Then we'll put them to the fearsome mosquito box test." Daniel wiggled his eyebrows at me.

The next morning, which was Sunday, Daniel came early to my father's house. Most of our party was going to fly to Kitale in the western part of the country, which was where my father's family was from, but my mom had made my father promise I would take no flights inside Kenya, so he and I were going to drive. Daniel wanted to come with us, because he thought he would get a better sense of the country looking out a car window. "I'll ride in the back with the mosquito boxes," he said. "I have to keep an eye on their temperature."

My father drove, and I sat beside him, feeling awkward, not knowing what to talk about. He pointed at landmarks and told me about the history of the country, how it was a British colony, all about the Mau-Mau rebellion when Africans killed the British in their homes, and then about the independence movement and the various troubles Kenya had in moving toward democracy. Daniel asked questions and made comments until he said at one point, "Jet lag is catching up with me. Wake me up when we get to the Great Rift Valley." Then he lay down on the back seat.

My father went on talking. Now he talked about the roads. "This is a fine highway, but as soon as you get off the main road we are left with dirt roads that are full of ruts that wash out in the rainy season. To drive anywhere takes many hours. Sometimes when you drive through a village, you will see young boys filling ditches in the road with dirt so you can pass. They hope the drivers feel so grateful they will give some money. What the travelers do not know is that as soon as the car passes, the boys start to dig out the ditch again so they can fool the next person to pass."

I was too angry with my father to pretend to be interested in roads.

After a while my father looked in the rear-view mirror. "I would like to talk to you, but I wonder if your friend is really asleep."

In response, Daniel gave a soft rumble of a snore.

"Nala, my lioness," my father said. "Alice tells me I have been a fool and a coward. She says I should have told you a long time ago that we were married and had children." He looked over at me.

I stared straight ahead, not saying anything.

"I feel so bad about your mother," he said. "She was willing to give up everything, to embrace a young country, to embrace me." His hands tightened on the steering wheel. "And then we failed her. The medical care here . . . I still wonder whether, if the accident happened in her own country, the care would have been better and she could have walked again."

"People get paralyzed in America," I said.

We drove on for about a mile, and then I burst out, "Why didn't you come home with her?"

"I couldn't get a visa," he said. "Not at first. And then her family didn't want me."

"Who cares what they wanted?"

"We wrote letters and we talked long distance. What could I do in America, in North Carolina, an African immigrant? Rake the lawn, be the man who carries groceries to the car? Your mother said it was God telling her our marriage was not meant to be."

"God?" I asked, incredulous.

"Your mother said God had carried her through the accident and brought her safely home. She said her life had to take a new direction now, and that having me around would only be a reminder of what she had lost."

"She doesn't talk about God now," I said.

He sighed. "Your mother is a woman of great courage," he said. "I think she wanted me to go on with my life, so only one life would be ruined."

"Her life wasn't ruined," I said angrily. "People think that. They think a bad accident ends everything. Well, it doesn't. My mother has me. She's a librarian. She has friends. People love her."

"I know," my father said. He took his eyes off the road and gazed at me. He repeated, "She is a woman of great courage, and she is still my strong, good friend."

I turned my face away so he couldn't see the angry tears running down my face.

nineteen

Mr. Bowen had reserved a big round conference room at the Kitale Club for a hundred or so members of my father's family. The setting sun lent an orange glow to the neatly tended lawns and the dancing wavelets of the swimming pool. To the west, Mount Elgon cast a purple shadow as the sun dropped swiftly behind it. "This is where the English people used to party," my father said. "Kenyan people were only the servants."

Nick set up a computer at the entrance of the dining room and registered people's names as they entered. My father stood beside him, greeting each person, taking the men's hands in both of his, lifting the little children high. The women's dresses were splashes of color, and the men wore white shirts and dress slacks or torn sweaters and shorts. My father seemed to know each person's name. He explained to Nick how they were related, and he introduced me to each of them: "My beautiful American daughter, Nala." Sometimes he spoke a few words to an older person in his native language, Luhya.

The staff glided around offering hors-d'oeuvres and beverages like at a wedding reception. Then my father asked the adults to sit at tables so Professor Munyole could address them. The children had been jumping up and down at the parents' sides, asking if they could go swimming, and at that point Mr. Bowen asked Nick to go act as lifeguard. Most of the boys just tore off their T-shirts and jumped shouting into the water, while the girls trailed off to a changing room outside. "You can join them if you want," my father told me, and I did want to, but my bathing suit was still in the car, and besides I was shy, so I shook my head and found a seat at a table with Daniel. While Professor Munyole spoke, waiters set up a buffet dinner around the edges of the room.

Professor Munyole stood at a podium at the front of the room. He began by thanking Mr. Bowen and Drossila Pharmaceuticals. "We have asked you here because some members of your family have a special feature," he said. "You could call it a special talent, or a special power."

A boy, running in dripping from the pool, shouted, "A superpower!" and slid across the smooth floor toward his mother. She grabbed his arm and shushed him.

Professor Munyole barely paused. "Some members of this family are not bitten by mosquitoes. We believe this is because your skin manufactures a substance that does not smell good to mosquitoes."

"Some people stink!" the same little boy called out. This time his father took him by the arm and marched him back toward the pool.

"If we can find out what this compound is," Professor Munyole continued, "we may be able to make it in the chemistry lab. We may be able to make it in large quantities and provide it to people to use on their skin. In this way, we may be able to fight malaria and other mosquito-borne diseases."

A woman raised her hand. "Mosquitoes do bite me. I have had malaria three times. Why should I be here?"

"You will help us find the true ingredient," Professor Munyole said. "Members of the same family are similar in many ways, so many of your skin compounds will be the same. You will help us find what makes the people who repel mosquitoes different from you. What compounds do they have that you don't?"

A man asked, "What do we have to do? Is it dangerous?"

Professor Munyole said, "Today, during dinner, you will come up one by one and put your hand into a box of hungry mosquitoes, to see if they will bite you. It's safe. None of the mosquitoes have any disease. Then we will ask some of you to come to Nairobi for further testing."

"What do we get for this?" one man asked. "To come to Nairobi, we have to miss work."

Mr. Bowen moved in from the wings, smiling. "Drossila will pay for your trip, will put you and your family up in a fine hotel, and will cover any forfeited wages."

An older woman heaved herself to her feet. "That is all a very good thing," she said. "To make something that drives away mosquitoes is a very good thing. How will you get this thing to all the people?"

"We'll make it available in all the general stores and pharmacies," Mr. Bowen said.

"You will sell it? Or will it be free to the people?"

"Ooh," Daniel said beside me. "I like this lady."

Mr. Bowen's smile thinned. "We have to charge to cover the cost of manufacturing and shipping," he said. "The chemistry, the packaging, these things don't come free."

"Yes, I see," the old lady said, nodding her head. "And who will get this money that comes from what-you-call-it, the compound that comes from our bodies?" She waved a hand, indicating all the seated people around her. "This compound that you will sell all over the world?"

I looked around for Nick, before I remembered he was outside being a lifeguard.

Mr. Bowen's face had no smile now. "Some of the proceeds will go to jobs here in Kenya and in other places. Any profits will go to the stockholders of Drossila." He drew his eyebrows together and glared at the crowd. "That's how capitalism works. And because Drossila makes money, we are able to make grants to support scientific research and education in Kenya."

Now my father got to his feet and went to stand between the professor and Mr. Bowen. "Drossila already sponsors the education of three Kenyan medical students every year," he said. "The company is financing a new research laboratory at the University of Nairobi." He turned to look at Mr. Bowen. "And most recently, Drossila has agreed to provide funding for three village clinics here, buying new refrigerators and microscopes for each one."

Mr. Bowen jerked his chin back in what I was sure was surprise, and then he smiled a pinched smile and said smoothly, "Yes indeed. We were happy to make this pledge. The best health care comes from a combination of research, manufacturing, education and local care. Drossila is proud to support all levels of health care betterment."

My father's smile shone, and he clapped his hands. "And now," he said, "let's call the children and eat."

"Did my father just play a trick on Mr. Bowen?" I asked Daniel.

Daniel swung his hair so that the beads rattled. "I'd say your father just saved Mr. Bowen's bacon," he answered. "Want to come help me set up the mosquitoes?"

We set up the boxes in the corner next to Nick, and one at a time, families came up from the tables to try their luck. First we asked them if they'd ever had malaria, or if mosquitoes liked to bite them. After they signed a form saying they consented to the test, we took their temperature and then had them put their hands in the box.

"But what if someone has malaria and doesn't know it?" I asked. "Like what if they're in that period between fevers where their temperature is normal, but they still have parasites in their blood? Won't our mosquitoes spread it from one person to another?"

"That's a really good question," Daniel said. "I'm glad you're thinking about the safety of our subjects. But it should be all right for two reasons. First, once a mosquito takes a blood meal, it won't bite again for at least a few days. Second, remember your malaria life cycle. It takes ten to fourteen days for the malaria parasite to change inside the mosquito to a form that can infect a new person. The parasite also has to move from the mosquito's stomach to its salivary glands. By the time that happens we'll get rid of these mosquitoes and be using new ones."

After that I felt better about the evening. If people were scared or reluctant, I went first, showing them how easy it was. It was funny. Some people said mosquitoes never bit them but they had gotten malaria anyway, which I was pretty sure was impossible. One teenaged boy said, "I think I have malaria right now. See how I am sweating?" Him we let stand aside. None of the people were too happy about putting their arms in the box, but they went through with it so they could hurry back to their big family reunion dinner.

My father brought one elderly lady to the corner and said, "Nala, this is your grandmother."

The old lady had eyebrows as black as my father's, but slim and curved where his were thick and straight. The skin of her face was smooth even though she only had a few teeth left. She squeezed both my cheeks in her hands and wobbled them. "So beautiful!" she said. "So strong and beautiful!"

I guess she was strong too, because mosquitoes didn't bite her.

People reacted in different ways to the mosquito test. When mosquitoes didn't land on him, the boy who had been so noisy thrust both fists in the air and leaped side to side, chanting, "Yes, yes, yes! Stronger than mosquitoes, yes, yes yes!" When mosquitoes landed on them, the children usually squealed, and some of the little ones started to cry and buried their faces against their mothers' blouses. Usually the men, once bitten, pulled their hands out quickly, sometimes with a curse. The women were more likely to leave their hands stoically in place until Daniel told them in a soft voice they could pull free.

A tall, thin man in a white shirt and khakis who had been watching from the poolside door came over to be tested. He looked about thirty, and he wore glasses that made his brown eyes look as wide and trusting as the giraffe I had fed in Nairobi.

"Name?" Daniel asked, checking Nick's list.

"Oh, you don't have me on your list," the man said. He put his hand into the box, and mosquitoes landed on it.

"Okay, I can see mosquitoes like you," Daniel said.

"They like me and love my children," the man said, staring at the mosquitoes furring his hand.

"You can pull your hand out," Daniel said. "Now, what did you say your name was?"

"Jackson," the man said. "I'm not family, just a friend of Robert's." He still stared at his hand, not moving. Then he looked at me. "Are you enjoying your stay? What are you most hoping to see while you're here?"

Surprised, I said, "I'd like to see flamingoes."

"Flamingoes are very beautiful," Jackson said.

"Pull your hand out, brother," Daniel said. "You're going to be covered in welts." He tugged on Jackson's elbow, and Jackson pulled out his hand and stuck it in his pocket. He made his way to one of the tables and began talking to the other people there.

Daniel gazed after him. "Why did he do that, if he's not family?"

"He probably just wanted to know," I said. "I thought he looked sad."

It took more than two hours to test everybody. Every once in a while, Daniel suggested that I take a break and get some food, but I didn't want to. I saw my father moving from table to table, smiling and talking, reassuring people and asking about their jobs and farms and animals. I saw that he was working, smoothing things over, getting them to trust what was happening. This was my science project too. I was going to stick by Daniel's side and make it work.

By the time we finished the last table, my face and neck were tired from smiling and nodding so much. The waiters were closing the pans of food, but other people at our table had loaded plates for Daniel and me: roast beef, those flat Indian breads called chapatis, the stuffed fried packages of dough called samosas, French fries (which they called chips), and lots of green vegetables and carrots. The food was kind of cold, and the rice pudding they had for dessert was slimy. I didn't eat very much.

"Too many people for you?" Daniel asked.

"Too many relatives," I said. "I'll never be able to fill out that chart."

Daniel laughed. "The pedigree chart? We'll work on it together. Nick got lots of information, and your father seems to know them all pretty well."

My father eventually made it around to our table. "You two did a good job. Everybody tells me my daughter has such dignity."

"I bet that means I don't smile enough," I said.

"Oh, Nala," Daniel said, "stop putting yourself down."

"My sister Naomi has an extra bedroom in her house," my father said. "But she has dogs that bark all night and a loud television and a rooster that starts crowing at four in the morning. I think after our long drive you both deserve hot showers and soft white sheets, so I've reserved you rooms here at the Club."

Daniel scooted his chair back. "No need for that, sir. I can just curl up in a corner somewhere."

"Nonsense. You and Nick will share a room. We need our scientists well rested. The two of you will be keeping guard over Nala. Tomorrow we visit the hospital."

"We have to go to the hospital?" I asked.

Daniel said, "We want to check blood smears on the people who say they've never had malaria. Sometimes people might be harboring a low-grade infection and not even know it." He turned up his hands. "If they have malaria, we won't be so interested in their skin compounds. For research, it's always better to double check."

"Besides, lioness," my father added, "we thought you would like to see the hospital, in case you want to come back here as a doctor someday."

His smile, so proud and indulgent, really bothered me. *No,* I thought, *you don't get a perfect daughter after abandoning her and her mother.* I said, loudly enough to make people at the next table turn their heads, "Fat chance. I got a D in science."

 **twenty**

"You didn't get a D in science," Daniel scolded as he dropped my duffel in front of the door of my room. The rooms at the Kitale Club came in pairs, in cabins beyond the parking lot. Nick, after promising to swim with me in the morning, had already holed up in the room he'd be sharing with Daniel.

Daniel continued, "You got a D on one assignment because you had integrity. You wouldn't put your name on bogus data. But you know what? You and I are going to write a paper together about an extended family where half the members don't attract mosquitoes. We're going to work out the pedigree and then we're going to figure out the chemical. Your name is going on the paper right alongside mine."

"All I've done is get born with some weird trait," I said.

"And followed it up with your father, and shared that information, and learned all about malaria, and traveled across the world to make introductions. We couldn't have done this project without you. Besides, I'm going to make you do a lot more work before you're through, starting with those pedigrees."

An embarrassing question came into my head: How old would Daniel be by the time I turned eighteen and could legally marry? I looked down so he wouldn't guess what I was thinking.

"Why are you so down on yourself?" he asked. "You're such a fantastic . . . person."

"You were going to say kid," I accused him.

"Person. Almost eighth-grader."

I burst out, "My dad doesn't even want me to stay at his sister's."

"Oh, Nala," Daniel stepped toward me, starting to open his arms, but then he fell back. No hug. "It's not like that at all."

I felt foolish for laying the drama on so thickly. "Maybe not."

Daniel waited as I carried my bag in and closed the door behind me. "Double lock it," he said through the door.

I peered out the peephole, which made his nose look extra big. "Because of al-Shabaab?"

"Because I said to."

I double locked the door.

I got up before either Daniel or Nick and decided to go swimming by myself without waiting. I walked barefoot across the graveled parking lot, into the clubhouse and through the big lounge with its TV and fireplace, to double doors leading to the golf course and pool. I walked through dew on the grass, over the sidewalk, past a man laying towels on the chairs. The early light danced on the surface of the water. I dove into the water and let it flow over me, so fresh and cool it seemed to wash away all my fretting and confusion.

Swooping underwater with nobody else around is like flying.

When I climbed out, the attendant handed me a towel, and I dried off and wrapped it around me. I was pretty sure I shouldn't go in to breakfast in a swimsuit, but I didn't feel like changing yet, so I sat at a poolside table. When a waiter came, I ordered orange juice and coffee and charged it to my room.

Before too long, Daniel came to sit across from me, wearing a green and black dashiki, which is a big baggy African shirt, and carrying a newspaper in his hand. "Raid on al-Shabaab Camp Comes Up Empty," the headline read.

Daniel said, "I thought you were still sleeping. No answer when I called your room. But here you are, ahead of us all."

I laughed. "I wanted to swim with all those other kids last night, but you made me work instead."

"The life of a dedicated scientist," Daniel said.

Nick came out the double doors, unshaven, with his hair wet from the shower. He flung himself into a chair and glanced over at my place. "Hey, I didn't know you drank coffee," he said.

I gave my most dignified smile. "There's always a first time."

Daniel ordered us omelets and funny triangular doughnuts with no holes in them. We had slices of papaya on the side. When Daniel caught me making a face at my coffee, he got all three of us some of the Kenyan milky tea. After we finished eating, Daniel and Nick sent me back to change before my father arrived to take us to the hospital.

We drove slowly, sharing the road with bicycles, these incredibly crowded little buses called matatus, and a flock of skinny sheep, past little roadside shops that looked like garden sheds. Most of them seemed to be selling the same few things: soda, candy, a couple of kinds fruits, cookies, tea, and eggs. Kitale Hospital looked like something a not-very-creative giant had built with building blocks—a set of parallel cement-block buildings only one story high, connected by covered walkways. We entered the outpatient clinic, whose waiting room was already full of pregnant ladies and children wriggling in discomfort on their mothers' laps.

A man in a white coat came to greet us. "I hear you want to use our micro lab, Minister," he said to my father. "We have a very busy morning clinic."

"We won't interfere," my father said. "You have two microscopes, yes?"

"Not as fancy as you're used to in Nairobi, I'm sure," the doctor said. "Or in America," he added, looking Daniel up and down. His forehead wrinkled at the sight of Daniel's dashiki.

"If you could just show us one we can use," Daniel said.

The doctor waved us into a side room where a young woman bent over a microscope. Daniel introduced himself. "What do you end up seeing here mostly?" he asked her.

"Malaria, typhoid, ameba," she said. "Various parasite eggs."

"Do you have some malaria slides I can show my young colleague?"

She motioned to a pile of glass slides. "Put them back when you're done."

Daniel put the slide under the microscope and adjusted it for me to see. I had a hard time seeing through the microscope. It seemed out of focus, and then for some reason I kept seeing my own giant eyelash. At last I made out some pale, brownish-red disks. "Red blood cells," I said.

"And what do you see inside them?" he asked me.

"What am I supposed to see?"

"Let's start with what you see," Daniel said. "What good does it do if I tell you what to see? You are an independent person."

I told him that some of the red cells were messed up, broken. Some of them had blue gunk in them. One of them had a blue ring, like a sapphire engagement ring. "That's a classic sign of malaria," Daniel said when I showed him. Daniel kept changing the slides, making me describe what I saw.

Then my father suggested we take his blood. Daniel put on gloves and picked up a small, sharp piece of metal. "This is a lancet," Daniel said, and briskly he stabbed my father's finger and squeezed out a drop of blood. He showed me how to collect the drop on a glass slide, and how to smear it with another slide. "We call this a thick smear," he said. "When it's dry, you look carefully to see if you find any sapphire rings in your father's red cells."

That's how we spent the morning. My father led relatives into the lab, and Daniel pricked their fingers, and first I and then Daniel searched their slides. I didn't see any signs of malaria.

"Maybe we're just not looking enough," I said. "There was that kid who felt feverish. I wish we had his blood."

"Go look," Daniel suggested. "Maybe he's out in the clinic waiting room."

I found my way back to the clinic entrance. Now the line of people waiting wound out the door. An old man leant on his cane, holding a hand to his chest. A woman with swollen ankles stepped stiffly forward, moving as if her hips hurt. A couple of children gazed up at me from seats on the floor. I didn't see the young man.

When I returned to the lab, I told Daniel, "Those people are going to be waiting for hours, and some of them look really sick."

Daniel turned his head from the microscope to look at me. "It's tough. Not enough doctors, not enough medicine. And Kenya's a relatively rich country, for Africa."

After we had looked at slides for about twenty of our test subjects, my father talked the doctor into letting us tour the rest of the hospital. It was different from the hospitals I'd seen when my mom had to go in for a urinary infection or something. Wide old hallways opened onto rooms where a rank of iron bedsteads stood in a row. Whole families gathered around a bed, sometimes having picnics. "The families bring in food for the patients," my father said. "Usually they have to go buy the medicines at the pharmacy themselves."

My favorite room was the nursery, where four babies with smooth brown faces slept all wrapped up like sausages in their bassinets. In a rocking chair against the wall, a mother sat nursing another baby, who was even tinier than the rest.

When we had finished our tour, my father asked Daniel if he could manage without me for the afternoon. "Nick can help you," my father said. "Nala and I are going sightseeing."

"Is it okay?" I asked Daniel. "Will I still get to be on the paper?"

Daniel laughed. "Of course you will. Go ahead. Child labor is illegal, you know."

My father took me to a reptile park. Crocodiles snapped at the bottom of one stone pit, and in another, snakes writhed and slithered. It was awful. "Can't we maybe go see some flamingoes?" I asked him.

"Flamingoes?" My father pushed himself up from the stone barricade where he'd been leaning. "Tell you what, on the way back to Nairobi we'll go to Lake Nakuru. We'll see the flamingoes on the lake—hundreds, thousands of flamingoes. And then we'll go on safari and see some other animals too, impala and wildebeest and zebras and cheetahs."

"Were there zebras where we lived when I was little?" I asked.

"A couple," he said. "We lived at the edge of town, and sometimes the zebras would browse around the garden. And there were zebras and impalas near the airport."

"I knew it," I said.

Instead of flamingoes, we went next to an outdoor museum that had model houses from different tribes. "You see, this is a Luhya house," my father said. "A round house with mud walls and a thatched roof."

Living in one of these would be like staying in a castle tower, I thought. "Did you grow up in a house like this?"

"Yes. And as soon as the children are old enough, maybe five or six years old, their parents build them a house of their own, right next door. Instead of your own room, you get your own house."

I wanted to stay in my very own round house. I asked, "Is this what my Aunt Naomi's house is like?"

"No, I'm sorry to say hers is a boring old rectangular house made of concrete." My father hesitated. "Daniel says you might like to stay there. I can trade places with you if you like. But there's no swimming at my sister's house."

"Maybe just the very last night," I said. I liked the feeling he gave me, that he wanted to please me, that I had some power over him. Then I thought of Alissa getting stuff from her divorced parents, playing them off against each other. I hoped I wasn't turning into Alissa.

"That sounds good," my father said, and he led me on to show me a typical Pokot house and then a blocky Njemba one with a flat roof. He said, "Tomorrow, maybe I can take you to see the forest antelope, the sitatunga, that swims in the swamp. Do you think tomorrow Daniel Wright will let me have my daughter to myself?"

My father wanted to spend time with me, just me alone. I said, "Probably, if I work on the pedigrees—you know, the family trees—tonight."

twenty-one

I did work on the pedigrees with Daniel after dinner, while my father and Nick played billiards in the sports bar. Daniel and I spread sheets of paper on a low table and taped them together. Daniel read off Nick's computer, and I drew careful lines on the paper, showing how everyone was related, up to my father's second cousins, who had the same great-grandfather he did, and their children, who were my third cousins. I colored in the squares and circles for people who didn't attract mosquitoes. If we hadn't tested someone, we put a question mark in their circle. For people who had died, we put a little cross.

"Look at this," Daniel said. "What do you see? What can you conclude?"

"There are filled-in circles in every branch." I traced back along the lines. "I mean, we can't test my great-grandparents, but some of my dad's second cousins have the trait too, so probably they all got it from one of their parents, who got it from one of their grandparents, and back and back further than that."

"I agree," Daniel said. "This trait has been around a while. And do you see how if either parent has the trait it gets passed to about half the children in each generation? That's what we expect with a dominant trait. You have a fifty percent chance of inheriting it from your parent who has it."

"Huh," I said. "I wonder if my children will repel mosquitoes. But I guess it doesn't matter, because I'll just be able to rub Essence of Nala onto them."

"Maybe," Daniel said.

"Only maybe?"

"First we have to isolate the chemical."

"Which you will do," I said. "I believe in you."

"Then we have to learn how to synthesize it, how to make it from scratch."

"That sounds good. Instead of, like, locking me up in a steam room for life and harvesting my sweat."

"And even then, it's perfectly possible it won't work."

"Why not?"

"Well, what if Essence of Nala evaporates so quickly it only lasts on the skin for five minutes? It would be okay for you, because you're constantly making more of it, but it wouldn't work out of a bottle."

"Oh." I felt crushed. Maybe my superpower was going to be something I couldn't share at all. "Do you think that's what will happen?"

"I don't know." Daniel stood up. "Want a ginger ale? And let's challenge your father and Nick in billiards."

The next morning, when I came out of my cabin already wearing my bathing suit, someone was waiting for me. "Good morning, Nala," he said.

It was Jackson, the man who looked like a sad giraffe. "Good morning," I said. I wondered why he was there.

"Your father sent me to get you in the car. Today he's taking you to see flamingoes."

"I thought today was the swimming antelope," I said.

"Things got moved around," Jackson said. "He knows how much you want to see the flamingoes."

I hesitated. "I thought today was just my dad and me."

He laughed easily. "I'm just delivering you. Then you'll have your father all to yourself."

"Oh." I considered. "Shouldn't I wait to tell Daniel and Nick?"

"Your father settled it all with them last night," Jackson said. "Come, get dressed, it's best to see the flamingoes early in the morning."

"Someone should have told me," I said crossly, but I went back in my room and changed into longish pink shorts and a tailored, short-sleeved shirt. I grabbed my phone and went out again. Jackson smiled to see me.

Outside, he opened the back door of a battered gray car that looked old and kind of tired. Its exhaust pipe dragged on the ground, and the rear bumper sagged. It was really different from the car that had taken us to the university in Nairobi, and Jackson looked nothing like a chauffeur, but I slid in anyway. Jackson got in the driver's seat and checked me in the mirror. "Remember to wear your seatbelt," he told me.

I settled back in the seat and watched the scenery. We passed lines of newly planted trees and fields of corn, or maize as they call it in Kenya. After a while, I said, "Shouldn't we be there by now?"

"Be where?" he asked.

"At my Aunt Naomi's house, to meet my dad."

"Oh, no, you misunderstood," Jackson said. "We are meeting your father at the lake, not at the house."

Something in the way he said it made me uneasy. "How far is it to the lake?"

He made a face. "Fifteen minutes."

I heard a click and looked at the door. The door lock was down, and I hadn't locked it. Maybe Jackson had locked it just for my safety, but

I eased my cell phone out of my pocket and looked for the automatic dial.

Just as I pressed my father's number, the car jerked to a halt. Jackson swung around in his seat and grabbed my wrist, squeezing so hard I cried out. My hand fell open, letting the phone fall onto the floor.

Jackson somehow vaulted over the seat back and landed beside me. His foot stamped down on my phone the moment it began to ring. I squirmed backward and twisted around to pull the door lock up, but it wouldn't budge. I yanked at the door handle, but it didn't move. Jackson put an arm around my neck and yanked me back toward him. I felt him lean down and reach for my phone on the floor, and I heard the ringing stop.

"You are coming with me," Jackson said in my ear. "Now we will take a few precautions. And you will obey me, so you don't get hurt. Understand?"

No cars were coming from either direction. I whimpered, choked, and tried to nod.

"Okay, then." He relaxed the hold on my neck enough that I could breathe. "Now give me your hands."

He tied my hands behind me with a cotton scarf, and then he wrapped another scarf around my eyes. When I tried to open my eyes, I saw light come through the yellow and orange pattern of the cloth, but I couldn't see around the edges. *How will I see the flamingoes?* I thought for a wild moment, before I realized that of course there would be no flamingoes. *And Jolene will never get her pink feather.*

"Are you from al-Shabaab?" I hated the way my voice trembled.

"You are afraid of al-Shabaab? Good. I am from al-Shabaab." He pushed me away. "I can tell how frightened you are, because you've wet yourself. Now you will lie down here on the seat and be quiet while I drive, because you know we of al-Shabaab could happily shoot an American girl like you."

He pushed me down, and I lay with the rough upholstery pressing against my cheek. *But he looked so nice,* I thought, *like a giraffe.* He got out of the car, and then I heard him stamping his foot and a crushing sound. With a sick feeling I realized he was destroying the phone my father had given me. Now I had no connection to anyone. My breaths shortened and grew faster, and my stomach wobbled with fear. The front door opened and the car started up again. Jackson turned on the car radio, which began to play African music. I didn't know people from al-Shabaab liked music, but it settled me down just a little.

Dear God, I prayed, *I'm no good at this praying stuff, but if you exist, please rescue me now.* I didn't have much hope. God would have to be a real pushover to save someone who only prayed about once every five years.

My mind burned with fury at myself for agreeing to leave the hotel with Jackson. How could I have fallen for his line? My mother had trusted me to be smart. I thought of Daniel not finding me at the poolside, my father panicking when he saw my unanswered call and tried to call back. I imagined him calling the police, calling my mother. *I hope he doesn't call her,* I thought. *I hope he finds me first.* I prayed again and tried to quiet the thumping of my heart. *Think, think.*

The car pulled off the main road onto a road that bumped and jolted. In books, people who are kidnapped memorize the road so they can help the police later. "We turned right onto a dirt road," I would say. But after how long? I couldn't tell if moments were passing, or hours. I tried counting seconds to myself and taking note of turns in the road. I lost track pretty quickly, but somehow I felt a little calmer. Surely Jackson wouldn't bother to take me so far away if he meant to kill me.

"Your name isn't really Jackson," I said.

He didn't answer.

"Mosquitoes like your whole family," I said.

No answer.

"If you drop me off here, I promise not to tell anyone what happened," I offered.

No answer. I couldn't think of anything else to say, so I went back to paying attention to the road. At one point we bucked sharply through a couple of ditches, and I heard children's voices demanding something. It must be one of the villages my father had mentioned, where kids dig ditches and then fill them in, demanding payment from passing motorists.

I had always wondered how loudly I could screech if I really tried my hardest. Now was the time to find out. I opened my mouth, jerked myself upright, and screamed, "Help! He's kidnapping me!"

The car jolted forward with a roar and bucked its way along the road. "You just made a stupid choice," Jackson said. "Now I have to put a gag on you, and you will be very uncomfortable."

He came in the back door with yet another scarf and tied it across my open mouth. Then he returned to the front seat and started up again. The scarf covering my mouth made me feel panicky, as if I wouldn't be able to get enough air in through my nose. Perspiration beaded my forehead and dripped onto the seat. *No mosquitoes will come in this car for weeks*, I thought crazily. The scarf around my mouth grew wet with drool. Still, I was surprised it wasn't worse. Shouldn't a fanatical al-Shabaab killer at least hit me for screaming like that?

Unless he was just waiting for some more secluded place to start beating me.

twenty-two

I don't know how long I lay in the back of that car as it fumbled its way over bad roads. From time to time I sobbed silently, longing for my mother and wondering what she would do without me. My nose ran too, and along with the drool from my gag, the tears and snot made a wet spot grow under my face. But eventually, scared and uncomfortable as I was, I dozed. I dreamed I was flying into a steamy cloud, and then I woke with my cheek squashed against the fabric of the seat, with the sound of scratchy hymns in my ears and the smell of sweat and urine assaulting my nose. What was an al-Shabaab killer doing listening to Christian music on the radio?

Finally, the car took an abrupt turn to the left and stopped. Jackson's voice broke through my stupor. "When I open the door, you will stay completely silent."

His door opened, and a moment later, I heard my door open too. His hand closed on my arm and I slid toward the door. My back and neck were stiff, and as I tried to stand I stumbled. Jackson pushed me ahead of him. Bright sunlight filtered through my blindfold and then dimmed as we stepped through a doorway. The floor felt soft underfoot. I smelled onions and charcoal. A woman's voice gave a soft exclamation of surprise.

"I brought her," Jackson said. "We'll keep her in the other house."

A slim hand took my arm and led me outside again. Jackson's footsteps sounded behind me. We passed through another door.

"Sit," Jackson said.

I folded myself onto the floor.

"I'm going to untie your hands," he said. "But if you try anything, I'll tie you to the wall and you won't like it at all."

When he loosened my hands, I rubbed my wrists and shoulders. My joints felt like I was about sixty years old. I tugged at the gag, and somebody untied it. "Can I take off the blindfold?" I asked.

"Just a minute," Jackson said, almost as if he was a store clerk serving me. Again, his tone made me think he wasn't as fierce as he pretended. Jackson spoke in his own language to the woman, who I imagined was his wife, and I heard her leave. Then I heard something sliding beside me, and Jackson said, "You can take it off, but I don't want you moving this curtain for looking outside."

I slid the blindfold up off my head and looked around me. I sat on a woven mat near one side of a round house. The curving wall was uneven and whitewashed, and the floor under the mat was packed dirt. Thin curtains made of green patterned cloth hung over the two windows. A pile of blankets lay stacked against the far wall. In the dim light that filtered through the curtains, the roof rose to a central point, and woven roof thatch filled the gaps between wooden ribs. *A Luhya house*, I thought.

Someone tapped at the door, and Jackson opened it a crack. A slim brown arm reached in, holding something blue and neatly folded. Jackson shook it out. It was a blue dress.

"You can change clothes," Jackson said. "Then you can wash your clothes." Sure enough, in another minute, the woman passed a plastic basin full of soapy water through the door. Then Jackson left, walking with the dipping gait of a giraffe, and locked the door behind him.

For a while I sat holding my knees and shivering, but in the end I wanted to get clean, so I pulled the dress over my head and undressed beneath it. The dress was baggy and shapeless and hung below my knees. I dunked my shirt, which was still clean, in the water and wiped myself down before dumping my wet underwear and shorts in the water. Scrubbing them calmed me down a bit. *I'm going to get through this,* I thought. But then I was left with wet soapy clothes and nothing to do.

"Are you finished?" Jackson asked at the door. His arm handed in another basin of water, with no soap this time. I rinsed my clothes and wrung them out, and then I flung them up over the curtain rod to hang and drip dry. I felt strangely detached, as if some other girl were doing this, not me. *I'll just do this and not think about what comes next.* I set the two basins out beside the door as if I was putting out the trash.

"Are you hungry?" a woman's voice asked softly at the door.

"Yes."

Nothing happened for a while, but then the door opened and the woman, who must have been Jackson's wife, came in with a plate of food. She was slim and no taller than me, and her face looked sad. She kept her eyes looking down, and her hair was jumbled in a tangle on top of her head. *I bet her husband beats her,* I thought. *That's why she's so sad, and if I can get her on my side we can escape together.*

She handed me the plate without speaking and withdrew through the door. She wasn't the one who closed it, so I realized Jackson was standing there, guarding the door when she went in and out, so I wouldn't be able to make a break for it.

There was no fork. The food was cold ugali with bitter greens of some sort. I rolled the ugali in my fingers and took as long a time to eat as I could. Already I had the feeling time was going to pass very slowly here.

The next big event came something like an hour later when the woman returned to collect the plate. "Thank you," I said, hoping to get her on my side. "It was delicious," I said. "See, I cleaned my plate."

She didn't answer, keeping her eyes down. Her dusty feet wore battered-looking flip-flops. "I said, "My name is Nala. What's yours?"

When she didn't answer, I said, "I need to go to the bathroom."

She pointed at a bucket against the far wall and said, "Use that."

I wrinkled my nose and shuddered. "I can't. Don't you have a toilet?" When she hesitated, I crossed my arms over my belly and moaned, "It hurts."

The woman shook her head and backed out of the house. I heard her talking to her husband outside. Jackson called to me to put the blindfold on, and then the door opened again and the woman led me out of the house and across a sunny yard. I thought I heard chickens clucking, and then a door creaked open and I felt a doorstep against my ankles. I stepped up into the stinky darkness.

"You can take off the blindfold to go," Jackson's voice said.

It was a latrine. Flies buzzed around the seat. Lines of light shone between wooden slats. I sat down and did my business while trying not to breathe through my nose.

"Cover your eyes before you come out," the woman said.

As she helped me down the step, I said again, "What's your name?" When she didn't answer, I had an inspiration. "Then I'll call you Mama." I thought maybe she couldn't be cruel to someone who called her Mama. "Why are you kidnapping me, Mama?" I asked. "I've never done anything to hurt you."

Without answering, she led me back into the hut and closed the door behind me. I pushed the blindfold off again.

And then I sat there, scared and confused. By this time I was pretty sure Jackson wasn't from al-Shabaab, but I couldn't figure out why he had taken me or what he might do with me. To distract myself, I memorized the pattern on the curtains. I traced out shapes in the mat under me. I tried to remember all the characters from every Harry Potter book, and I closed my eyes to remember them the way I first imagined them, not the way they turned out in the movies. It didn't work very well. Imagined thoughts and images kept leaping in to disturb me—my father yelling at Daniel and Nick, my mother weeping with the phone in her lap, my half-brother Adam smiling a secret smile of satisfaction. Jackson approaching me with a raised machete. Vultures picking at my dead body abandoned on the savannah.

I lay on my stomach to dull the thumping of my heart, but it seemed to shake my whole body, so I turned over onto my back on the mat and peered up at the thatched ceiling. If only I could fly up there, maybe I could squeeze out where all the thatch met at the peak, and then, scratched but free, I could spiral up into the clouds and set off flying back across the map of Kenya to my father.

It bothered me that even in my imagination I didn't know which direction to fly.

Thinking about flying made me realize that I really ought to be working on my escape. In movies, in books, prisoners escape. First I checked the windows, being very careful so Jackson wouldn't catch me looking out. I peeked around the green curtain hanging over one window. Behind it, the window was thick and framed with iron. I tapped on it. I was pretty sure that even if I threw a safe at it, it wouldn't break, and all I had was a plastic bucket. Besides, the window was crossed with actual iron bars. The other window was the same. So much for that.

The hut had a dirt floor. The obvious approach would be to dig my way out. I crawled around inside the walls, looking for a place where the dirt was soft, but I didn't find one. So I just chose a spot on the side opposite the Jacksons' main house and pulled the mat away from the wall. I scratched at the dirt with my fingernails. It felt like someone was ripping my fingernails right out. Little puffs of dust rose, but after what seemed like forever I had only dug down about an inch in an area smaller than a plate. I tried to be optimistic. Say an inch an hour, or more like three hours, because the hole had to be a lot wider. So if I dug twelve hours a day I could get down four inches. Maybe I could get through a tunnel four feet long, so that was only about twelve days. I'd break through at night and slink off across the fields. By daylight I'd reach some village or main road and get help, as long as no leopard caught me and Jackson failed to track me down first.

Okay, it sounded really hard, but possible, if I kept scratching away at the dirt twelve hours a day. But the ground kept getting harder, and my fingernails felt like someone was sticking needles under them. I bit my lip and blinked away tears. Blood rimmed my fingernails. It was no good, it hurt too much. Next meal, I would have to try and get a fork from Jackson's wife. I brushed as much dirt as I could off my hands and sucked on my fingertips to soothe them. Then I got a blanket and lay under one of the windows, where a thin line of light fell across my body.

The rest of that day was the longest I had ever spent. I never knew a person could be so scared and so bored at the same time. My thoughts ran in circles, and no matter how I tried to hold onto the good thoughts—Jolene singing in assembly, my mom letting me lick the brownie bowl, running through the woods in cross-country—other, more threatening images broke in. There were a lot of vultures in my thoughts. Off and on I dozed. I got hungry. I had to pee again, and this time I used the bucket. I heard children playing outside, but I was too scared to pull the curtain back again and look.

Eventually, another meal came. Ugali and bitter greens, and a tin mug of milky tea. "Mama, can I have a fork?" I pleaded. "In America, I always eat with a fork."

She gave a quick shake of her head and looked away.

This time she didn't return for my plate. Gradually, the room grew dark. I used the curved edge of the mug to scrape away at my hole, but I couldn't really see what I was doing, which discouraged me. Finally I pulled a couple more blankets off the pile against the wall and wrapped myself in them. The hours crept by, marked only by the distant barking of dogs and one crazy rooster who didn't seem to know the time. *Courage, lioness,* I told myself, but in my head the letters of "lioness" rearranged into "loneliness." I buried my face in the blanket and tried to let myself cry, but my weeping was dry, and no tears came.

twenty-three

*I*n the morning, Jackson brought me a piece of paper and a pencil. "Write this, so your father can see your handwriting," he said.

I didn't tell him my father doesn't know my handwriting, because we use email. Instead, I obeyed, and wrote, *Dear father, please do just as this letter says, and I will come back to you safe.*

Jackson said, "Now sign it."

"But it doesn't say what he has to do!"

"That will be added on the bottom."

On the top I wrote *Wednesday,* and then I signed, adding curlicues to my name. Slowly, I said, "Mr. Jackson, my father doesn't have a lot of money."

Jackson pulled his lips back into a mirthless smile. "Ah, so your father is the first member of our government not to take bribes? Maybe so. But for sure his friend Bowen is rich."

"They're not really friends."

Jackson ignored me. "I'll tell you how to get rich. Sell drugs at high prices to people who can't say no. People who need the drugs or they'll die." He snorted. "Hold their children for ransom. 'Your child will die if you don't pay me so much money for this drug.' But these same people will call *me* a criminal."

"I'm not Mr. Bowen's daughter," I said. "Why should he pay for me?" As I said that, I imagined Alissa in my place. If she'd come along, Jackson would have kidnapped her instead. She'd be the one crouching in this corner in a shapeless dress with her hair a mess. I had trouble picturing her messing up her manicure by scratching at the dirt. But Alissa would have been too smart to go with Jackson in the first place.

"He'll pay," Jackson said.

It was true that Mr. Bowen was really rich, and it would look bad for his company if he didn't rescue me. Hope flickered in my chest.

A silence followed, and to break it, I asked, "What will you do with the money?"

"Money!" he shouted. "Can money for one person make up for injustice to a whole people?" He snatched his glasses off and glared at me with the eyes of an angry giraffe. "Can money bring back from death even one small person?"

I shrank backward, shaking my head. "So what will you ask for?"

"Free drugs for all people of Kenya. Free drugs from Drossila for every Kenyan person."

I thought of Mr. Bowen's answers to the woman at the banquet, all about costs and profit, and I felt like Jackson had just blown out my hope lantern. "He won't do that."

Jackson shrugged his shoulders. "Then he will receive little pieces of you, mailed in an envelope."

I gulped. But then I told myself that Jackson wanted to terrify me, and that the only way to fight back was not to be terrified. "An envelope, huh? Sounds like pretty small pieces, all right. Maybe you could start with my fingernails."

Dumb! Because of course Jackson's glance went straight for my fingernails. I didn't want him to see my bloody fingernails and guess about my digging, so I closed my fists over my thumbs. "And my hair," I said quickly. "Locks of hair are very popular."

Jackson stared at my hair with his big sad giraffe eyes. I decided to try and get him off the subject altogether. "What one small person?"

He gave a little jerk and lifted his head, sticking out his jaw.

"I have a little brother named Benjamin," I said, surprising myself. "He doesn't walk yet."

"Our Esther walked," he said. "She said *Dada* and *Mama,* and she loved cows. She played beneath their bellies and they didn't mind."

"You have cows?" I asked.

He gave himself a shake and glared down at me. "No questions!" He grabbed up my letter and folded it.

I babbled, "I am so so sorry about your daughter. I wish I could meet her and hug her and carry her around. Please let me help your wife today. I can do the dishes or wash clothes. I promise I won't run away." Now why did I say that, I wondered, and did a promise to a kidnapper count? "Please don't leave me all alone."

He stood smoothing the folds of the letter. "I'll come back later," he said. As he locked the door behind him, I was left wondering whether that was like your parent saying "We'll see," or whether it was a flat-out no.

Eventually, he did come back. He let himself in, and on a rope he led a black-and-white dog with one blue eye and one brown one. "Here, pat him. Let him smell you," he said, so I knelt on the mat and welcomed the dog with open arms. I guess he found a lot to smell, since I'd only rinsed myself off that once in a couple of days. The dog thrust his nose into every part of me. I just kept patting him and murmuring, "Good dog." So I was going to have a dog to keep me company.

But finally Jackson pulled on the rope. "Now this dog knows your smell. If you try to run away, he will follow you and find you anywhere. Then we will not be so nice to you."

Hmm. I noticed Jackson didn't mention chopping me into little bits again.

"Put on your blindfold," Jackson said.

In the main house, Jackson let me take the blindfold off. To my surprise, I saw that his wife was now carrying a baby in a purple scarf hung across the front of her body. The house was another round, thatched house, a little bigger than the one where they kept me. Two tall sets of shelves set off one slice of the room. Peeping past the curtain into that slice, I saw a double bed, neatly made, with a cardboard box full of blankets on the floor beside it. A mosquito net hung over the bed. The larger section of the house contained a low coffee table and a couple of battered couches, along with a bookshelf that held dishes and a few books and papers. Spoons, but no forks, stuck out from one jar, and another held pencils and pens. Dangling from the doorframe hung a pair of soft pink baby shoes. Not really a lot of stuff. I couldn't see where they cooked or got water.

Jackson tied the dog to a chair and went out. He was a terrible kidnapper, I thought. I could knock over his little wife and baby, pick up a carving knife for self-defense, take the dog with me and head for the road. If I knew where the road was. If his little wife was as frail as she looked. If the dog would come along. And what would I do with a knife, anyway?

I decided to bide my time. "How can I help, Mama?" I asked.

She handed me a broom, which was just a bundle of long plant fibers tied together. I dabbed at the floor with it until she took it back and showed me how to use it properly, bending at the waist and swinging her arm from side to side as she slowly advanced.

It turns out it takes a long time to sweep a dirt floor, even when it's covered with a mat.

After that, Jackson's wife let me eat some ugali and wash the ugali pot, which had been soaking in the plastic basin. Each time she went out, she locked the door behind her, and I cuddled the dog until she came back. I figured I wanted the dog on my side, and besides, though rather smelly himself, he was affectionate, and he wriggled in pleasure when I patted him. Pirate, I called him, because of his funny eyes. It occurred to me that he was half black and half white like me, only patchy, and I wondered how people would look at me if I had one brown and one green eye.

Jackson's wife brought in a big plastic basin of soapy water, which she set on the floor in front of me. Then she slipped behind the curtain and emerged with an armful of clothes. "You wash these," she said, without looking at me.

I lifted the pieces of clothing one by one into the basin. It looked like one change of clothes for each member of the family. Three T-shirts, different sizes. A boy's shorts and a man's. A little dress and one more my size. Various underpants, but no socks. Either Mrs. Jackson was really good at keeping up with laundry, or this family didn't have a lot of clothes.

"Where do the other children sleep?" I asked.

Mrs. Jackson gave me a blank look. "In their house," she said.

I thought about that. "Where are they now?"

"At school," she answered in a dull voice, and then she lifted the back of her wrist to her mouth and looked at me with wide eyes. She probably wasn't supposed to talk to me.

"Isn't school over for the summer?"

She shook her head, dropping her glance again.

School. There would be people there, adults who would report a kidnapping. I wondered if the dog knew the way to school, and my little flame of hope flickered again. "How long have you had this dog?" I asked.

Mrs. Jackson shook her head. "He's not ours." She lifted off her sling and laid the baby down, then knelt beside me and demonstrated how to scrub more vigorously, using the brush. The baby cried weakly. For a while Mrs. Jackson ignored him, but finally she went to pick him up and let me work.

When I had scrubbed so long I ached, I rocked back on my heels and rested my arms. "I'm so sorry about your little daughter Esther."

Mrs. Jackson put her face against her little boy's belly, and said in a muffled voice, "He told you?"

"Just a little. He said you lost her. He didn't tell me any details."

She held the baby against her and rocked. Then all at once the words came tumbling out, fast but toneless. "She was two years old. The mosquito nets are old, and there was a hole in the one over her bed. At first she was just fussy. Amos went to find someone with a car to take us to the clinic. The medicine they gave her didn't work, and she kept getting hotter and hotter. She held her head and cried.

"We borrowed the car again and took her to the hospital. They told us the malaria must be too strong for the medicine. There was another medicine but it was expensive and they had run out of it in the hospital. Amos went to buy the medicine while I waited with Esther. He had not enough money. He promised the chemist he would get the money soon. He even offered to trade the car, which wasn't his. The chemist told him to go outside and beg for the money, but instead my husband just grabbed the medicine and ran. He ran back toward the hospital, but the police caught him and threw him in jail. Esther and I waited for him, waited. He didn't come, and after some time, my baby began to shake and throw her body around. The nurses rushed up and said it was a seizure. They put her on an IV drip, but it was too late. She died, hot in my arms."

Feeling sick, I left my basin of water and went to put my arms around Jackson's wife and baby. Only now I knew he wasn't Jackson, but Amos. I also knew I could never knock his wife down or threaten her with a knife, even if I got hold of one. "What did they do to Amos?" I asked.

She put her hand on my forehead and gently pushed me away. "His cousin, the one with the car, came and bailed him out. Then the judge dropped the case."

"What about the chemist?" I asked. "Did anything happen to the greedy chemist?"

She turned her back to me, still rocking the baby and talking in that curious flat voice. "The chemist is the police chief's brother-in-law. The police chief told us if anything happened to the chemist, my husband would go to jail for a long, long time."

I stood there with my arms hanging down. Stupidly, I said, "But now you have another baby."

She shook her head. "I didn't want another baby, but I was pregnant. What could I do? What can any of us do? I don't want to live."

She frightened me. "But your children, your other children!"

"That's what Amos says. But in this world, maybe they will die tomorrow."

"Let me go," I said. "Let me go, Mama, and I will get my father and Mr. Bowen to help you."

She shook her head again. "Amos has his plan."

I thought for a minute. "What was the name of the medicine Amos couldn't buy?"

She shook her head. "I don't remember these long names. It was two medicines mixed together. But I remember, because Amos keeps telling me, the name of the company that makes it: Drossila."

twenty-four

Early in the afternoon, the man I still called Jackson in my mind returned from wherever he was working to take me back to my own house. He wore rubber boots caked with mud, and he had a swampy smell with an undersmell of manure. After a whole morning of actually talking to someone, I felt strangely giddy. I stood patiently as he blindfolded me, as if we were preparing for some birthday game. The blindfold hardly seemed serious after I'd been looking out his windows all morning. Jackson didn't seem like a very experienced kidnapper, so I decided to check on his progress.

"How's it going? What does Mr. Bowen say?"

He grunted. "None of your business."

Feeling the soft ground underfoot and the sunlight filtering through the blindfold, I tried to decide how much I could talk to him. "Of course it's my business. Wouldn't you want to know, if you were me?"

When he didn't answer, I went on, "What I don't understand about kidnapping is how you do the exchange, you know, person for ransom, without getting caught." This really had been worrying me. On TV shows, the handoff always seems to end in an exchange of gunfire. A person could get hurt.

Jackson grunted as if to say yes, he'd been worrying about that too. I prodded further. "Did you send them the letter?"

To my surprise, this time he actually answered. "No. I phoned a newspaper, and then I threw away the phone."

"I don't think you need to throw away the whole phone," I said. "You can just change the sim card."

By now we were back in my own house, and Jackson pulled my blindfold up and narrowed his eyes at me. "Why are you giving me advice?"

"I want to hurry this along." I raised my chin. "For your information, this isn't how I planned to spend my summer vacation."

He shook his head slowly.

"So what did they say? My father and Mr. Bowen? How do they call you back?"

"They must put an advertisement in the newspaper. I will see it tomorrow."

Tomorrow! Maybe tomorrow the wheels would start turning, and in another day or two I would be free. I thought I could stand to wait that long. "I hope it goes well," I said politely.

Shaking his head, Jackson backed out the door.

Back in solitary confinement, my mood plummeted. When I heard laughter and running footsteps, I peeked under the curtain at Jackson's children coming home from school. The little boy chased chickens around the yard, and the girl sat at the outside table writing in her school notebook. The dog, Pirate, came out of the main house and trotted toward me with his nose almost touching the ground, until I heard him snuffling at the door. A moment later, I spied him helping the little boy chase chickens. Pirate danced around the boy with his tail wagging so hard his whole body wriggled. Next he greeted the girl, poking his nose into her leg and her lap. He seemed to really like those kids, the traitor.

I lay down on my mat, stared at the pointed ceiling, and thought. I told myself not to be terrified; Jackson wasn't as fierce as he tried to be. But I was trapped and bored and worried about my parents. I imagined my mother crying, waiting by the phone in America. She would feel so helpless with no way to reach me.

A scrape of footsteps on pebbles sounded near the window, and I jumped up and put my eye to the crack between the curtain and wall. The little boy stood peeing against the side of my house. On impulse, I twitched the curtain open and made a face at him. He jumped and squawked, zipping up his shorts as he darted back to his sister's side. I drew back into the darkness of the house, but I watched the girl take her brother's hand and bravely approach. When she got close enough to see inside, I raised my head, pushed back the curtain, and gave her a little wave. She jumped, clutched her brother's hand harder, and stood her ground. We stared at each other for a moment, and then she ran to the main house, dragging her little brother along.

As soon as the children disappeared, I remembered how Jackson had warned me about moving the curtain, and how he had promised to punish me if I disobeyed. I huddled in the corner, awaiting his heavy footsteps and his angry voice. I actually trembled, but he didn't come. I wondered what he was telling the children—maybe that I was a crazy aunt he was sheltering and keeping secret from the world.

I didn't hear the children outside the rest of that afternoon. Neither Jackson nor his wife brought me supper that night.

Already I felt as if I had been away from my family forever. Jackson had taken me on Tuesday; it was only Wednesday when I scared his children. Night meant twelve hours of darkness fidgeting on my blanket, hearing weird noises. I was pretty sure a single lion couldn't break into my house, but I imagined I heard a whole pride of them padding around the house, looking for the door. I was hungry and thirsty and I had to pee, but I really didn't want to use the bucket in the darkness. I had seen some pretty big spiders during the day. There might even be snakes. A black mamba might be wrapping itself around the edge of the bucket right now.

To keep away thoughts of lions and snakes, I tried to imagine myself as a princess in a high tower, waiting for rescue, like Rapunzel. Only my hair would never be blond or straight enough to hang out a window. I tried to imagine Tom Vledecky riding up on a red-gold horse to save me, maybe carrying a nice big cheeseburger. But even in my imagination he was awkward and kept falling off the horse. Better Daniel, rigging up some kind of fantastic ladder out of wood from the scrubby acacia trees around the farmyard. Nick would run around following Daniel's directions.

Then I imagined my father and Nick and Daniel and people from Drossila trying to find me, questioning the staff at the hotel, searching the roads. If they asked the boys who filled ditches what cars they had seen, maybe the boys would tell them about me screaming in the back seat of a gray car. Nearby, they would find the white cellphone smashed and lying among the weeds. Then they would identify the tire tracks and hire an expert Kenyan tracker, maybe one of those tall, painted Maasai tribesmen. Surely they would be here to rescue me in no time.

But no rescuers came. The next day, and the next, I helped Jackson's wife in the house. Sometimes, when the baby lay in a corner crying weakly, I asked her if I could hold it. She shrugged as if she didn't care. He was a boy, light and droopy in my arms. His eyes were dull and he didn't lift his head. Besides cuddling the baby and sweeping up, I ate ugali, took blindfolded trips to the outhouse, patted Pirate, and peeped under my curtain at Jackson's two children playing in the yard after school. All day Thursday I was quiet and meek, but Friday afternoon, when Jackson walked me back to my house to lock me up, I asked him for an update.

"I sent them your letter," he said. "But every day the newspaper ad is the same: Let us talk to her. They leave a phone number."

"So let me call them!"

"No. It's a trick. They'll put a trace on the phone. The CIA will track me like a terrorist and send a drone to kill me."

I wondered if that was true. Jackson was my kidnapper and I should hate him, but I didn't like the idea of him exploding in a drone attack.

"Let me call someone else," I suggested. "Someone they don't expect. Like my mother in America."

"Call overseas? How do we pay for that? I don't trust the international operator."

This was crazy. He was just too scared to end this thing. "Let me call the newspaper!"

Jackson paced around my little prison-house, turning from time to time to look at me. "This is not my only problem. How can I make sure Drossila keeps its word? They say, 'Yes, we agree to provide free drugs,' and I let you go, and then what?"

"You need a contract," I suggested.

"And what solicitor will write one for me?" he asked. The corners of his mouth turned down. "I don't have the money to bribe a man of law not to go to the police."

I didn't know how to answer that. I said, "This is too complicated. Just ask for money ransom like a normal kidnapper. Ask for enough to buy medicine for your family for the rest of their lives."

Jackson gazed down at me through his glasses, slowly wagging his head as if I were a disappointment to him. "You should care for your people," he said. "All of us are important, all our children, not just one family."

He made me feel small, as if somehow I was not as good a person as he was, my kidnapper.

Jackson continued, "Drossila needs to prove their good will. They will have to distribute free medicine to all the clinics and hospitals in Kenya. Then I will let you go."

"Good idea," I said, though I thought it sounded complicated. "But let me call my father."

Jackson shook his head and went to the door. Watching me, he shook his head again, and then he exited and locked the door.

At first I felt relieved. At least we had a plan, one that would lead to my freedom. But before long, I began to realize that Jackson's plan was a bad idea for me. Distributing free medicine might take weeks, during which I would be locked in a dark hut listening to spooky sounds and waiting for a CIA drone to strike and maybe miss its target and hit me instead.

Then there was the niggling feeling that my friendly conversations with Jackson made me a traitor. A kidnapped person isn't supposed to help her kidnapper. That was weak and cowardly, like a princess helping the witch who kept her captive in a tower. A kidnapped person should try to escape. And for two days I had forgotten to try and smuggle a spoon out of the main house. At this rate, I would never dig a tunnel.

I watched beside the curtain as the two older children came walking home from school. Pirate ran up to greet them, jumping up to try and lick their faces. The boy, who held a stick in front of him like a lance, pushed Pirate aside so he could charge imaginary enemies. It almost made me laugh to think that little boy was the closest person I'd seen to a knight riding to my rescue. And it almost made me cry to think how I waited for them to come home from school, but they carefully averted their heads and wouldn't even look in my direction.

And then, as I thought about school, I began to form a plan.

twenty-five

*T*he next two days were Saturday and Sunday, and the children didn't have school, which meant I didn't get out of my prison at all. Jackson's wife brought me food and took away my bucket, but all I got to do was pace around my hut and sometimes try to work a little on my tunnel. I got it down to about six inches, which was pathetic. Most of the time I ended up crouched by the window peeking around the curtain at the life of freedom outside.

The children had their own round house next to their parents', which I thought was pretty cool. Both mornings, after they ate breakfast in the sunshine, the little boy picked up a long, flexible stick he had left by his door, pulled on rubber boots, and went off with his father to work. He came back by lunchtime without his father. I guess half a day of work was plenty for him. Meanwhile the girl helped in the garden or chopped vegetables at the outdoor table by the pump. When the boy came back, his sister wrinkled her nose at him as if he stank and made him wash off his muddy boots.

They never came to my door, though they must have known I was still there. I thought about tapping on the window to get their attention, but I had no idea what Jackson would do if I disobeyed him again—maybe starve me to death. So I just watched them. Then, on Sunday afternoon, the boy came over to pee against the side of my hut again, and he put his face against the window. For some reason, I drew back into the darkness as he did that. I don't think he saw me, but a little while later, I saw the girl writing in her school notebook. She tore out a page, looked both ways, and then crept over and slipped it under my door.

I ran to unfold it. *Hello*, it said. *We hope you feel better soon.*

Maybe their mother had told them I was a sick relation who needed absolute quiet to get well. Only they had written in English.

Whoever they thought I was, they wished me well. That made me choke up a little. If I had a pencil of my own, I would write back, *Help me, please. Tell your teachers I am Nala Simiyu and they need to tell Minister Robert Simiyu where I am.* But I didn't have a pencil, not even a stick. I tried to spit in the dust and make an ink of mud that I could smear with my finger, but it didn't work.

Then, finally, Monday came, and after Jackson left for work, the kids gathered up their schoolbooks. Tied to the pump, Pirate whimpered as the children set off for school. Not long afterward, Mrs. Jackson brought me to the house and brought Pirate in to watch over me.

My skin felt jumpy with my plan. Pirate, tied to a post, watched me with droopy eyes and a happy tail that thumped the floor. At every creak of the house or shadow crossing the window, I imagined Jackson coming back to check on me. But the truth was I didn't have to wait too long for my chance. Mrs. Jackson, with the baby in its purple sling, went outside, and the door behind her didn't click. She hadn't locked it, which meant either that she was just outside it and only for a moment, or else—I hoped, I hoped—she had just forgotten.

I waited a few moments and crept toward the door. Sure enough, I could lift the latch and even push the door open a couple of inches, but Mrs. Jackson and the baby were just in front, so I silently dropped the latch again and backed away. I tiptoed back to my work and tried to quiet my thumping heart by squeezing my fists shut on the wet clothes I was washing. I sloshed the clothes in the soapy water, peeking out the window as Mrs. Jackson gradually worked her way, weeding, to the back of the house where she wouldn't see the door.

I untied Pirate, which was hard, because the knot was tight and my fingertips still painful from all my useless digging. But I managed to get him free, talking to him all the while. "Okay, Pirate, you're not going to be chasing me, because you're going to be with me, see? And besides, you have an important job. I have a big treat for you. Here it is! Take a whiff of this. Lovely, stinky boy socks I saved for you. Don't they smell wonderful? Now, as soon as I open the door, you're going to follow this smell and find the boy, get it?"

Pirate wagged his whole body. I hoped he understood what he was supposed to do—take me to the boy, to school, where I could beg for help. Surely the teachers would report a kidnapping. Even if not, there was no way Jackson could keep me secret if hundreds of kids saw me.

We waited by the door. Pirate's tongue lolled, very casual looking, but my heart pounded. I pushed the door open an inch. It creaked. Whatever. It was now or never. I pushed it farther, and we slipped out. Quietly, I shut the door behind me, to make it longer before Mrs. Jackson noticed we were gone.

"Let's go, Pirate, take me to the boy," I whispered. I shook the sock in Pirate's face and then pushed his nose to the ground. He snuffled and followed his nose in a path that wound back on itself in tight circles. "No, Pirate, where did the boy go?" I don't know if Pirate understood me, but after what seemed like forever of aimless circling, he angled off along the path I'd seen the children take. A good sign. I kept my head low. Soon we were trotting.

The land was low and swampy, puddled in some spots, with tufts of ragged grass and reeds. The only little round houses I saw were distant, far across muddy expanses that looked hard to cross. Above the swamp, the path ran on a little ridge of drier ground. As Pirate trotted faster and faster, the vision of the school with all its responsible official adults rose more clearly in my mind. At the same time, I grew frightened, with a feeling I haven't had since I was a little girl—that someone was behind me, someone I would never see, chasing me but hiding whenever I glanced back.

Then Pirate stopped, nosed a bush, and yanked me down off the main path. Here a much narrower path, marked by boot prints, wound through the mud and faded. I didn't know if Pirate had caught scent of some delicious animal, or if maybe Jackson's boy had taken a shortcut across this field on his way to school. "Come on, Pirate, let's get back on the big path," I suggested. The ground, swampy underfoot, sucked at my sneakers.

Pirate kept pulling. Ahead of us stood a low wooden building in the middle of a green and muddy field.

"Bad dog," I said. "Take me to school."

But Pirate just wriggled his whole body as if he was pleased with himself. I tugged on his rope.

"Hey!" shouted a voice from the direction of the building. My heart stumbled in my chest. It was Jackson.

Pirate strained toward the voice. In a panic, I dropped his rope and ran. My sneakers squelched through the mud, and I ran the way you do in a dream, with feet heavy and uncoordinated. I didn't dare look behind me. I lunged up onto the path and ran as fast as I could in the direction I still thought must lead to the school. On dry land I was sure I was faster than Jackson would be in his big rubber books. If only I had kept up with my cross-country training in the offseason! "Help!" I shouted, with what breath I had left. "Help me, I'm kidnapped!" Soft, fast, footsteps sounded behind me, and Pirate rejoined me, running and leaping, dragging his rope, winding around my ankles so I had to jerk and dodge around him. My breath came in ragged rasps.

Then Pirate tripped me and I fell to my hands and knees. As I scrambled to my feet, Jackson grabbed my shirt and jerked me backward. His hand clapped over my mouth. A knee banged into my hamstring, and my leg buckled. Jackson's arm caught me around the waist, and his voice hissed in my ear. "You will be sorry for this."

I turned and clawed for his eyes, but he slapped my face so hard my head clanged. Tears ran down my cheeks. "Try anything, say anything, and I will beat you," he told me. "Now walk, straight ahead of me, straight home, silent as air, or you will know my fist." He twisted my arm behind me and gave me a shove.

Crying, gulping, I stumbled ahead of him. My head hurt, my arm hurt, and I was mortified to have failed, to be crying. Who would be so stupid as to try and run away in broad daylight?

Jackson's wife ran out of the house to meet us. Jackson yelled at her in his own language, and when she tried to reach for me, he knocked her away. Roughly, he shoved me to my own hut, opened the door, and thrust me inside. He followed me in and spun me around to see him. He held Pirate's rope looped in his hand. As he stepped forward, I fell back.

"You promised not to try to escape," he said. Light from the window crack, reflecting on his glasses, made his eyes blank. "Now I must beat you, and then I will tie you up." He grabbed my arm and lifted the rope. I closed my eyes and cringed.

The rope whipped against my legs, my back, my legs again. In fact, the rope was too thick and Jackson was standing too close to me to make it hurt terribly, so it was fear and humiliation more than pain that made me cry. Ten, fifteen blows, and I heard other crying beyond my own. The rope fell to the ground beside me. I turned and looked at Jackson, and even through my own blur I saw that his face too was covered in tears.

"Now I will tie you," he said. "Put your arms behind your back."

He tied my wrists with the rope and then tied the other end of the rope to a bar on the window. "Sit down," Jackson said.

When I sat, the rope behind me tugged my arms upward toward the window. "It's too tight," I said in a small voice.

He ignored my complaint and walked to the door. Just before he went outside, he said, "Now you will be alone."

twenty-six

Alone, my shoulders wrenched tight behind me, I sat in misery. I had been beaten and nobody cared. My face felt swollen and the welts where the rope had struck me burned more than before. I was thirsty and I had to pee, and I was stupid for having tried such a stupid plan to escape.

I heard the kids come home from school and heard them calling to their mother from the yard. Ordinary kids, who got to go to school and come home and be with their mother. I ached for my mother, wanting her arms around me, my head resting on her softness, her voice murmuring comfort into my hair.

Night dropped over me, complete lonely darkness. I couldn't hold my urine any longer, and I wet myself. Then I sat there, damp and aching and ashamed. Even when I tried to imagine flying, I couldn't lift off. Instead, I tried to focus on my mother, her pinkish-white face and the tone of her voice. "You're all right," she said to me. It's what she always said when I was little and fell or stubbed my toe. Once I argued with her. "I'm NOT all right. I wouldn't be crying if I was all right!"

"You're all right," she repeated. "In a moment you'll know it."

I was not all right. But instead of just feeling, I started to think. It was strange how guilty I felt, and I tried to figure out why. Because it was all my fault, because I went with Jackson to see flamingoes, because I broke my word to him and tried to escape. Because I was punished, humiliated, sitting in my own pee. I thought, *A person being punished thinks she's done something wrong.* That made me sit up a little straighter, and I scooted back a smidgen to relieve the pull on my shoulders.

I decided I needed to gather the people I loved around me to give me strength. I imagined Jolene here in my place, with her lower lip stubbornly stuck out. If she were tied up like this she would sing, sing so beautifully Jackson's children would gather round and Jackson's heart would melt. I'm a terrible singer, but I let some of Jolene's favorite songs—*Swing Low, Sweet Chariot* and *Hallelujah* and some songs by Adele—play in my head. Not as good as iTunes, but it helped. And then I thought of Nick. In my place Nick would be sitting here calculating how to make a deal, how to negotiate his way out of this.

That brought me back to something else my mother used to say, when I was little and kids were sometimes mean to me. "When someone is cruel, it's because they're weak," she said. "Maybe they're having some kind of trouble in their lives that makes them weak. You are the strong one."

Was Jackson weak? Was he in trouble in his life? He had lost his toddler daughter. His wife was so depressed she could hardly take care of their new baby. He had kidnapped me and he didn't know how to get rid of me safely. And now maybe I had attracted attention and the police would come for him.

That scared me. Maybe he would have to kill me and hide my body to get out of the bad situation he'd made for himself.

He cried when he was beating me. If he decided to kill me, he would cry a lot more.

"You are the strong one," my mother said, silently, in the black night.

I have to help Jackson, I realized. *I have to help get him out of his trouble, to save myself.*

In the morning, Jackson came to loosen my arms and give me some water. He wrinkled his nose at the smell of me. I stood up and rubbed my shoulders. "Mr. Jackson," I said, "we have to get this thing finished. Otherwise the police will find you."

He narrowed his eyes and drew back his head to look down at me. I thought he looked like a giraffe prepared to bolt.

"I know how you can do it," I said. "Let me call a TV station. We'll tell them to record my call so they can put it on the news. I'll say you'll let me go as soon as Mr. Bowen promises on TV that Drossila will give free malaria drugs to every person in Kenya."

"What are his promises worth without a contract?" Jackson asked.

"It's like my dad did at the Kitale Club. Mr. Bowen can't go back on a public promise, or everyone will attack his company. The TV recording will be there for anyone to see. He'll be trapped."

Jackson hesitated, and I pressed on. "Please, it's our best chance. And then you can take me back to Kitale."

He shook his head. "Not Kitale. They will catch me."

"Well then, somewhere. Somewhere safe, please."

"I know where I could take you," he said.

He astonished me. I wasn't used to grownups taking my advice, especially grownup kidnappers. But then he frowned again.

"You know too much about me," he said.

I said carefully, "I know your name is Jackson and you have three children." *Except your name is really Amos, and you work in a dairy, and you live in a marsh in a Luhya house.*

"What was the name of my little girl?" he asked.

"Naomi?" I said.

His shoulders relaxed. "I'll need to borrow a car," he said.

Jackson left me tied up, but more loosely, and after some time Mrs. Jackson came in with a plate of ugali and greens. *When I get out,* I thought, *I'm never going to eat ugali again.* It made a tasteless mass in my mouth, but when it fell into the hollow ache of my stomach, I felt a little better.

Then I waited, my stomach flopping every time I heard a sound outside, thinking it was Jackson come to get me.

The day stretched on, and I dozed, my dreams jumpy with TV cameras and angry giraffes. Then light fell across my face and Jackson's voice said hoarsely, "Get up."

He held a cell phone and as I watched, dialed a number. "You will say exactly what I tell you to say." He put the phone on speaker and held it in front of my mouth.

"You will say, 'I am the kidnapped girl, Nala Simiyu, and I want to be on the news. Record what I say.'"

A woman answered the phone. "KBC, please hold."

"I am the kid—" I began, but music interrupted me.

We waited. The background music was Simon and Garfunkel's "Mother and Child Reunion." My lower lip trembled.

"KBC, how can I help you?"

"I am the kidnapped girl, Nala Kisimu, and I want to be on the news. Record what I say."

A moment's hesitation, and then the woman asked, "Is this is a trick?"

Jackson shook his head. "Not a trick," I said, and then, with my voice trembling, "Please help me."

"Shall I call the police?"

"No, no! Record me. He wants me to be on TV."

"Just a minute." The woman sounded panicky. She shouted, "John, come here, it's the kidnapped girl, how do I record her?"

A man's voice came on, calm and deep. "It would work better if we call you back. Can you give us the number?"

Jackson shook his head again, violently, but I already knew the answer. "No, please just record me."

We heard a whir and a beep. "Go ahead, we're recording," the TV man said.

I repeated what Jackson murmured in my ear. I meant to please him by sounding scared and desperate, but it turned out I didn't have to act. Now that I was actually speaking to someone in the outside world—someone who knew about me, who seemed to care—I had to fight back sobs. "I am safe for now, but this is what has to happen for me to be freed. Mr. Steven Bowen of Drossila Pharma, Pharma—" I stumbled over the word but pressed on—"has to go on the evening news and announce that all its drugs will be given free to any person in Kenya that needs them. For diabetes, for pneumonia, for malaria. Any sickness, this year and forever. That is the price."

I took a breath and leaned back, but Jackson pushed the phone closer to my face and hissed more words at me. Voice trembling, I repeated, "He has to go on the news tonight or I will be killed and fed to hyenas."

"But wait," said the man at the TV station. "We might need a little time. Let us talk to your captors and hear what they have to say."

Jackson shook his head again, and I repeated, "If he does this tonight, I will be released in a safe place tomorrow."

Jackson pulled the phone away from me and turned it off. He took out the sim card and stuck it in his pocket. "Now," he said, "we will see."

 **twenty-seven**

Jackson wouldn't really kill me and feed me to the hyenas, I told myself. Not a man who cried while beating me.

But I wasn't totally sure. And if Mr. Bowen decided to call his bluff, why should Jackson ever let me go?

Then I began to imagine that Mr. Bowen would make his announcement but that Jackson would miss it somehow. I had never seen a television in his house. How terrible if Mr. Bowen made his promise but Jackson killed me anyway. How would he do it? Would he borrow a gun? Hit me over the head with a shovel? I sat holding my knees and shivering. Now that there was a chance I could be freed, I was more frightened than I'd been during the whole week I'd been a captive. What if Jackson was right and the CIA had traced the call? Would they send a drone or the Navy Seals? I listened for the chopping of a helicopter rotor.

Jackson's daughter sang in the yard. His son came over and peed against the side of my house again. School was out, and evening was on its way.

I had a water bottle and a plate of food, and because I was no longer tied up, I could use my toilet bucket. The urine had dried on my shorts, and although I was still hungry and stinking and aching, I knew I should feel better, but waiting made me feel as if I had drunk a hundred cups of coffee. All my nerves were firing with little electric buzzes. I did jumping jacks and commandos. I ran in place with my knees jolting as high as possible. Looking at my water bottle, an old beer bottle, I thought about breaking it and using a jagged piece with the bottleneck attached to work on my tunnel hole. But that was stupid. Tomorrow I'd either be free or—

Tomorrow, I told myself firmly, either I'd be free or I'd go back to my digging. No sense to risk making Jackson angry now.

By the time darkness settled, I hadn't heard from Jackson or seen his wife. I wrapped myself in a blanket and clutched my knees. As I had in the car when Jackson first snatched me, I prayed.

"Look, God, I know promises are shaky things. But if you let me get free I promise I will try, really try, to be a good person. Honor my father and mother, not steal, not talk back, be kind to others. Oh, please enter Mr. Bowen's heart and soften it so I can be free."

As usual, God didn't answer. I wondered if my mother had prayed to be able to walk again. I bet she did.

Oh, why did the nights have to be so long? And where was Jackson, and why didn't he tell me what was going on?

When the door to my hut opened, the air was still a gray half-night. It was Jackson, holding a scarf. My heart somersaulted. A blindfold, or something to strangle me with? But he stepped toward me and spoke softly, almost gently. "We are going on a journey."

"What did he say?" The words tumbled out of me so fast I could hardly understand them myself. "What did Mr. Bowen say?"

"He said that when you are returned unharmed, Drossila will begin to distribute the medicines."

I jumped up, punching both hands into the air, as if the two of us were comrades sharing some great victory. "Hooray!"

"Now," Jackson said, "You must wear the blindfold and keep silent as I take you to the safe place. Don't ruin everything now."

"Is it close by?" I asked.

"No. Far."

He led me into the yard, past where the stove and well stood, past the children's house and his own, to the side where the car had parked when we first arrived. But this door sounded different, and I had to crawl in to enter. The floor was hard metal under my hands and knees, until I found a blanket to rest on.

"Keep the blindfold on and stay silent," Jackson said. "Rest and relax. It will be a long ride."

The door closed behind me. It felt as if I was in the back of a van. That was smart of Jackson, not to use the same car.

A door opened, somewhere in front of me and to the right, and the van shifted a little as Jackson climbed in. He didn't speak to me. The van huffed into gear and moved backward, then forward. We were on our way, bouncing and jolting and swerving. This time I didn't even try to memorize the road. Helping the police catch Jackson no longer mattered to me. I just wanted to get home.

It was hot in the back of the van and very uncomfortable. No matter how I tried to spread or bunch the blanket beneath me, whenever the van jolted over a rut in the road I bounced into the air and came down with bruising force. My legs and bum got so battered that I tried squatting, letting my knees act as shocks to absorb the bounces. That killed my quads. I worked out a rotation, squatting, sitting, lying flat, to even out the discomfort.

And then with a last bucking movement we entered onto a paved road. I managed to spread the blanket evenly and lie on it face down, my head cradled on my arms. Silence, blindness. But we were getting closer. Cars honked and sometimes I heard barking or the shouts of people.

The van turned left, dipped and rose, swerved left again, and stopped. Jackson got out, and a moment later I heard a latch turn behind me, then a creak, and light poured around the edges of my blindfold.

"You can take off the blindfold now," Jackson said. "Come on over here."

I lifted the blindfold and scooted along the van floor to the back, where I hung my feet over the edge. Out there, a dusty courtyard milled with people. "Where are we?" I asked.

"A clinic. You will wait in line for half an hour and then you can ask for help. Understand?"

"Yes," I said. I didn't know if I could wait half an hour.

"All right," Jackson-who-was-really-Amos said. "Are you dizzy? Can you stand?"

I tried my legs. They seemed to work all right.

"Go over there." Jackson pointed. "Good-bye."

"Good-bye," I said.

"Think of the babies you're saving," he said, and then he closed the back door of the van. I tried to look past him to read the rear license plate, KUA something, but Jackson's legs blocked the rest of it. That was okay with me because wasn't sure I wanted to know the license plate number anyway.

I took my place in the line of people waiting, some dressed in suits or wearing jewelry, some dust-covered as if they'd walked a long way. Crying children with snot running down their faces, children with impossibly skinny legs or sores on their shins, babies drooping in their mothers' arms. Why should I wait? I was free now, and there was nothing Jackson could do to harm me. But for some reason I waited. Partly I didn't feel I had a right to go in front of all these sick people.

A nurse came around the courtyard, taking names and asking what brought us to the clinic. "My name is Nala Simiyu," I said. "I am here because I was kidnapped."

The nurse's hand flew to her mouth. "You are the one. You are safe, praise be to God! Come in, come in!" As other patients looked up to see who this healthy girl was, this light-skinned one who got to go before them, the nurse told them, "This is the kidnapped girl, and she is free!" Someone began to clap, and soon the whole courtyard rang with the sound of congratulations and clapping. I tried to smile at people, but their attention embarrassed me.

"I'm Betty," the nurse said. "Come back here with me." She took me into an office, sat me in a chair, and offered me a soda. "Wait a moment. I will bring the head doctor."

The head doctor came, and not long after that, the police. They gave me a clean dress and wrapped my filthy clothes in a plastic bag. Then the phone rang, and Betty handed it to me. It was my father. "Nala, thank God you're safe. We are coming as fast as we can."

The police constable was tall and thin and looked as if he could be Jackson's younger brother. He wrote on a pad as his superior, a heavy man in a suit, sat in a rolling chair and asked me questions that I felt strangely reluctant to answer. "His name was Jackson," I said, not mentioning the name Amos. "He was tall and thin, with glasses. The first time, he drove me in a gray car. The second time, I think it was a van."

"No, he didn't hurt me," I said. The police constable scribbled, and the heavy man in the suit raised his eyebrows at the welts on my legs.

"I'm very tired," I said. "I want to see my father. I need something to eat."

The police grunted and withdrew.

Betty brought me a plate of ugali and chicken pieces, and left me to eat it in peace. Right away I broke my pledge never to eat ugali again.

The next time the door clicked, I thought it was Betty coming back to get the dishes. But instead, the door swung back slowly, and then my father entered, pushing my mother in her wheelchair before him.

twenty-eight

My mother held my hand as the doctor examined me and Betty stood by taking photographs of all my welts and bruises on her cell phone. The doctor had thick white hair and a face furrowed with worry lines. When he finished, he said, "I see no harm but a few bruises, but I recommend we keep Nala in the hospital overnight for observation."

"Thank you," my mother said, "but we will observe her carefully at home. Before we go, is it possible for me to help her bathe?"

I stood by the sink and let my mother rub a soapy washcloth over my body. Sometimes I had to bend over so she could reach me. She said, "You're so much easier to bathe than when you were four years old. You'd always squirm off to a part of the bathtub where I couldn't reach you so you could splash and laugh."

"You're the one who got me through this," I said. "Whenever it got bad and I really needed to be brave, I thought of you."

She squeezed the washcloth against my collarbone. "Nala, I think that's the nicest thing you've ever said to me."

The police wanted to question me again before we left. We sat back in the nurses' office, me in my donated dress, with my parents sitting on either side of me, and the questions came. Could I give a detailed description of the man I called Jackson? Did he have another name? Did he have anyone helping him? What could I say about where Jackson kept me? What had I heard and seen?

I mumbled my answers, and kept back a lot of details, like Mrs. Jackson and the name Amos.

When the heavy policeman sighed and stood, helping himself up with a hand braced on his thigh, and the young constable folded shut his little notebook, and the two of them left, my mother asked me, "I feel like you're holding back, Nala. What's going on?"

My father said, "It's your duty to share everything you know with the police."

"Hush, Robert," my mother said. "Nala, tell us."

My words rushed out. "He's not really a bad man, Mom. His little girl died of malaria. He doesn't want other children to die."

My mother shook her head. "Kidnapping is not an okay way to make political change, Nala."

"He's a terrorist," my father said. "I want to find him and beat him the way he beat you."

My mother hushed him again. "Nala, there's a thing that happens when people are held hostage," she said. "They begin to identify with the people holding them captive. They feel sorry for them and start to share their opinions. It's a natural thing, when a person has so much power over you." She patted my hand. "Especially for a child."

I thought about what my mother said. "I tried to run away," I said. "And then when he caught me and punished me, I felt like I had done something bad."

"But trying to escape was brave and a good thing," my mother said. "Don't let him stay in your head, Nala."

My father said, "Kenya needs to capture this man and punish him. People need to know that force and crime will not be tolerated in Kenya."

"Tell you what," my mother said. "Let's go back to Kitale where you can rest. You can talk to the police again later."

My father let me be the one to wheel my mother back through the hallway, across the courtyard to the dirt parking lot where the van had parked. The constable stood there, and I pointed to the place the van had stood. "Look for tire tracks there," I said. "That's where we parked." I still didn't know if I wanted them to catch Jackson or not, but I thought the police ought to be more efficient.

A black limousine waited for us, and as we wheeled up, the driver's door opened and Daniel got out. "Hello, Nala," he said, and came over and wrapped his arms around me.

"You here?" I asked in amazement. "Did you stay out here all this time? Why didn't you come in?"

He shrugged. "Someone had to watch the car. Besides, I thought you deserved some private time with your parents." He gave my father an uneasy glance. "And I'm still doing penance for letting you disappear."

"It wasn't your fault," I said, feeling again the squeeze of shame. "I went with a stranger. You know, the guy who wasn't on the list, who said mosquitoes like his whole family. The one who looked like a giraffe."

My father helped my mother into the back seat, so I could sit next to her and rest my head on her lap. I felt her bony legs under my cheek. My mother patted my hair as Daniel drove, swerving around potholes, and my father gave directions, adjusted the radio, and looked back every couple of minutes to ask if I was all right. Everybody was treating me as if I was recovering from some terrible illness.

"How did you get here?" I asked my mother with a voice muffled by her skirt.

She said, "I flew to Nairobi. For the sake of your child, sometimes you have to put your fear aside." She stroked my hair.

"You flew!" I repeated in amazement, although of course she had flown. How else could she get here so fast? "That's the second good thing to come out of this."

"The second?" my father asked from the front seat. "What in heaven's name is the first?"

I sat up. "Dad! The free drugs from Drossila, of course."

"Oh, no," he said. "No, Nala. There will be no free drugs."

twenty-nine

"**B**ut why not?" I demanded, incredulous. "Jackson said Mr. Bowen agreed to the free drugs on national TV, and that's why he let me go."

My father turned to look me in the eye. "No company is going to give in to blackmail like that. Bowen said what he had to say to get you freed. He said if you were returned unharmed, he would do what the kidnapper asked. But if he goes ahead and does it, crazy people will start kidnapping people all over the world to get rich companies to give them things."

"Rich companies *should* give things to poor people," I said.

"That's not the way the world works," my father said. "Companies need to make money. They need to sell what they make, not give it away, so they can buy supplies and pay the people who work there. That's the reality, Nala."

I felt as if I'd betrayed Jackson. But he was my kidnapper, and I wasn't supposed to care about him. My head felt fuzzy and my father's words sounded so far away I wondered if there was something blocking my ears. I said, "But won't it make Drossila look really bad if Mr. Bowen made a promise on TV and doesn't keep it?"

"Oh, honey," my mother said. "It won't be hard for him at all. He said you had to be returned unharmed. You have bruises all over you, and you must have lost ten pounds. This man starved you and beat you.

He doesn't get a reward."

"But the reward's not for him," I said. I hiccupped back a sob. "It's for the people of Kenya, so their children won't die." I began to cry, and my mother pulled me down again, and I wept into her lap as she stroked my hair.

By the time we reached the Kitale Club, my mother's lap was soaking, but I had cried myself out. Children gaped as we unloaded my mother's wheelchair and my father lifted her into it. He wheeled her inside, with me keeping close to his elbow.

In the hotel lobby, Nick leapt up from a couch and ran over to hug me so hard I was afraid I would crack a rib. "I'm going to sleep with a sword in front of your door," he said. "No one will be able to sneak in and take you again." He held my hand and looked into my eyes. "I should never have slept in after I promised to swim with you."

My mother said, "I think it's time for all of us to let go of our guilt."

Without meaning to, I think, all of them, my parents, Daniel, and Nick, turned to look at me. For the first time I understood how frightened and guilty each one of them had felt, just like me. I took a deep breath and let it out, feeling some of that burden leave me. I felt I could rise onto my toes.

My father told me, "Nick has had the hardest job, sitting by the phone, talking to the Drossila people, the police, the news, waiting to hear anything, calling all of us as we searched."

"And now a hot bath for you," my mother said, "and then a long rest before dinner."

A bath is a good place to dream. Floating in the water is almost like flying, and in the water my bruises throbbed and then felt better, and more of my guilt floated away. My mother, waiting in the bedroom outside, never asked me to hurry. I used both bottles of shampoo and washed my hair three times.

When I came out, wrapped in a white fluffy robe, my mother had laid out my clothes, just as she did when I was a child. There were my pink flowered pajamas, wrapped in tissue paper fresh from the hotel laundry, and also a pair of light blue slacks and a blouse with a frilly neck. I looked from the pajamas to the bed with its white sheets and pile of fluffy white pillows inviting me to sink in. But I chose the clothes.

"I'd like to talk to Daniel," I said.

My mother raised her eyebrows but didn't ask questions. I picked up the clothes and went back into the bathroom to dress. When I came out, a knock sounded at the door, and I opened it to see Daniel waiting there, looking serious. We went down to the lounge, where he ordered a beer for himself and a ginger ale for me.

"What is it?" Daniel asked when we had found ourselves chairs in the corner.

"I'm so confused," I said. And then I tried to explain. I told him everything, but all in a jumble, all the things I hadn't told the police, about how Jackson was really named Amos, and about his wife and children, about the times he was cruel to me and the times we acted almost as partners. How I felt guilty when I tried to run away, how I felt in the end he almost trusted me. How depressed his wife was and how I feared what would happen to her if he went to jail.

Daniel just listened, making little grunts, sitting with his legs apart, his forearms resting on his knees, looking down at his clasped hands and nodding. When I had finished, he let the silence go on for a while and then said, "Yes, it's hard on a family when the father goes to prison." And all at once I wondered if he knew something personally about that.

I asked him if it was true that Drossila wouldn't—couldn't—keep Mr. Bowen's promise about the free drugs.

He sighed. "Companies have shareholders, members of the public who own shares, little bits of the company. Not just individuals, but big pension funds, like say the retirement funds for teachers or secretaries or steelworkers, all owning part of the company. All of these people have their savings in the company, so it's the company's duty to make money." He spread his hands. "If the company doesn't make money, the shareholders fire the president and hire someone who will change things."

Daniel stood and then sat down again. "And giving drugs away for free probably wouldn't even work. Who would get the drugs to the people? You could try to supply malaria drugs to all the hospitals, but what about the corner chemists where most people in Africa go to buy medicines? The chemist has a small business, like all these other little shops you see along the road. He buys goods and sells them for a little more. If you told him to give away medicine for free, why would he go to the trouble of ordering it and putting it on his shelves? It would cost him time and effort and gain him nothing. In fact some people would take his free medicine and sell it under some other name in the village."

Daniel's words made me feel both very tired and very sad. "So all the little Esthers will die unless their families are rich," I said. "All our work here will help people in America not get mosquito bites, but people here in Kenya will keep on dying, as if their lives don't matter just because they're poor."

"No," Daniel said. "We can't let that happen. There has to be some compromise, but it all depends on Mr. Bowen." His eyelids flickered. "He's been in Nairobi, coordinating with the national police and the television stations, but he'll be back here tomorrow. He was frantic when you went missing."

"He was?"

"It looked bad for the company, of course, and I suppose maybe he was worried about your parents suing him. But he kept saying how it could be Alissa, how he'd never forgive himself if you were harmed. He'll want to talk to you, Nala."

So then Daniel and I talked about what I could say. It was so complicated. Mr. Bowen would be like the police, just wanting me to tell him things that could help them catch Jackson. No, not Jackson, Amos. A man named Amos who worked in a dairy and lived in a swamp and had lost a two-year-old daughter named Esther. It was probably enough for them to catch him.

I sighed, sat back in the chair, and decided to change the subject. "How is our science going?"

Daniel shook his head. "You don't expect me to have focused on that, do you?" But he leaned forward. "It's exciting, Nala. More than half your father's adult kin are resistant to mosquitoes. More than half. That means there's been a survival advantage. The resistant ones are more likely to live to adulthood. Next summer I want to come back and test a whole lot more people, people not closely related to your father, but other Luhya people, to see how far back it goes. And if we can find the compound you emit, and maybe find the gene for it, we'll learn so much."

"Unless it's just some bacteria on our skin."

"But it won't be, not with you growing up in America and them growing up here. Or if it is, it's because of something genetic about you that attracts those bacteria that scare away the mosquitoes." He drummed his fingers on his knee. "No, the one thing that worries me is what I told you before, that whatever it is will be so volatile—will turn to a gas and float away so easily—that when we spray it on people's skin it will just fly away in half an hour and be no use as a mosquito repellant."

"But there's always the plant," I said.

He did a double take. "What plant?"

"Didn't I tell you? My father says the old people in his tribe know a plant that when you rub it on your skin makes you even stronger against mosquitoes. But it only works for people here in this part of Kenya." During my time lying on the floor of my prison hut, I had thought about what that meant. "So I thought maybe that plant juice has to act together somehow with whatever it is we put out in our skin."

Daniel stared at me. "Brilliant. Nala, I hope you're my research partner for a long time."

That's when I remembered the other question I'd been wanting to ask. "How old are you, Daniel?"

He laughed. "You mean, why do I act like such a kid sometimes? I'm thirty-two."

That crumpled me. Thirty was my upper limit. By the time I finished college he'd be more than forty, much too old for me to marry him. Instead, I'd end up stuck with some boyish boy my own age like Tom Vledecky.

But maybe I'd find someone better in college. I blurted out, with my face growing warm, "Daniel, someday when I get married, will you come to my wedding?"

He reached out and clasped my hand. "I'd be honored."

thirty

We ate dinner at a round table, me between my parents, Nick and Daniel across from us. "Just family," my father said, smiling.

When the waiter came to talk to us about what they were offering for dinner that night, I got down on my knees and begged him, "No ugali, please." The waiter widened his eyes, but my family members laughed. Then the waiter brought roast chicken and mashed potato and carrots and gravy, and I ate until my stomach hurt.

My father told me that tomorrow would bring more questions from police, the Kitale police this time, and an official visit from Mr. Bowen, and probably TV reporters, who were waiting outside the hotel right now. In fact, he said, maybe I could go wave at them out the door before I went to bed.

So I did, while the cameras flashed and reporters shouted questions, but I just smiled and shook my head. And then I slept in the comfiest king-size bed ever, with my mother beside me, and we snuggled in the night.

I slept until ten in the morning. When I woke, my mother was sitting in her wheelchair, sipping coffee and reading a book. She gave me a great big smile.

"I'm starving," I said.

"So am I. I wasn't going to go off and leave you alone."

"You should have ordered room service," I said.

The lobby was packed with police and reporters. Daniel was waving his hands, explaining something to the reporters, and Nick seemed to be holding off a pair of policemen. "Not yet," my mother told everyone as I wheeled her through. "Nala has to eat."

Orange juice and a thick slice of ham and an omelet and toast and milky tea. No coffee this time. I was through with pretending to be grown up.

And then Mr. Bowen came striding in and sat himself at our table. "Nala, thank God you're safe," he said. "I just got here from Nairobi. Welcome, welcome back." He took my hand in both of his, and I felt that his hands were shaking, in little shakes almost too fast to notice.

"Don't let me disturb your breakfast," he said, pushing back his chair.

"That's all right, we're finished," I said. "Actually, Mr. Bowen, I was hoping to talk to you, just the two of us."

My mother raised her eyebrows and wheeled her chair back a few inches the way she does when she's surprised. Mr. Bowen said, "Of course, but I wonder if you could do me a big favor first?"

"A favor?"

"Call Alissa with me. She's been worried frantic about you."

"But isn't it the middle of the night there?"

"She's waiting by the phone, hoping you'll call."

It was hard for me to believe Alissa really cared so much, but I agreed, and Mr. Bowen dialed. When the phone began to ring, he handed it to me. On the second ring, Alissa answered. "Hello? Dad?"

"It's Nala," I said.

"Nala, I can't believe it's you. Are you all right? Did he hurt you?

We've all been going crazy here. You were on the news, can you believe it? You're famous! When you get to school in the fall, you'll be so famous, people will be throwing themselves at you in the hallways and you'll never get to class!"

"I'm all right," I said. "I was scared sometimes, but he didn't really hurt me."

"You must be so brave," she said. "I mean, I was going to tell you about my summer, but it feels like nothing compared to what you went through." After that, she couldn't seem to think of anything more to say, and we hung up.

Mr. Bowen looked at me. His brown eyes looked thoughtful and maybe sad, and I supposed he'd heard how flat my voice was when I talked to his daughter.

I didn't want to go out to the lobby, among the reporters and the police. "Can we talk in a corner of the dining room?" I asked.

We moved to a corner near the glass doors looking out at the golf course. A man walked slowly around the edges of the green, cutting brush away with a long pair of shears.

"I wanted to talk about your promise on TV," I said.

His shifted his seat and tapped one foot. "It wasn't a promise, it was a ruse. A trick to get you freed."

"I get that. You can't keep the promise because you can't reward a kidnapper, and your shareholders won't let you bankrupt the company, and free medicine would be hard to distribute." I had practiced that sentence in my head, and it came out sounding very adult. Mr. Bowen looked impressed.

"But here's the problem," I said. "It's going to make Drossila look bad. Lots of people heard you make that promise. They'll think Drossila is being greedy and dishonest."

His lips pressed into a thin line. *Now he's annoyed*, I thought. And I remembered my mother: "Most people are good, or they want to be. Sometimes you just have to help them along."

"And there was my sacrifice," I said. "You know what kept me going? I kept thinking, *I'm here in Africa to help African people—my people—get free of malaria.*" I let my voice go shaky for a minute. "He, you know, Jackson, my kidnapper, he had a little daughter who died of malaria."

From Mr. Bowen's face, I could tell that he already knew this little bit of information. I said, "I kept thinking of my little brother, Benjamin. Or you could think of Alissa when she was two."

Mr. Bowen said, his voice hard, "What would you like me to do?"

I wavered. He sounded so harsh. *This is hard for him,* I reminded myself. *Let him be the one to find a solution,* Daniel had advised. "Find a middle way," I pleaded. "Something that doesn't hurt the company, but something that helps the people."

He hesitated.

I said, "I know finding a new mosquito repellant is no sure thing, but if it's going to have a chance, you need us, my family."

He gave a short laugh. "Everybody already had a fine banquet. They all agreed."

This was the trickiest part, the part that could make us enemies. "They may not agree to come to Nairobi for testing, not unless I convince them." I had talked this all out with Daniel, how to be a person of power. "Besides," I said, "I heard about this rare plant some of them know, that when you squeeze the juice from the leaves makes the repellant stronger. Daniel's really excited about it, but somehow I have to get them to share the secret with me."

Mr. Bowen narrowed his eyes at me. "Is this for real?"

"Cross my heart."

"Well. I don't exactly like being blackmailed again, young lady."

I thought about what Nick would say. "I'm thinking of it more as a business negotiation."

Mr. Bowen put his hands on his knees and stood. "Call it what you like. The first thing you need to do is to cooperate fully with the police. Then we'll see."

This wasn't going at all the way I'd hoped. Mr. Bowen's smile was gone, and he looked down at me through narrowed eyes.

I remembered how my father said I had dignity. I stood too, and offered Mr. Bowen my hand.

As Mr. Bowen shook my hand, some of the stiffness left him. "I know you've been through an ordeal, but you need to show me that you haven't just been brainwashed by your kidnapper. Drug companies like Drossila do a great deal of good in the world."

He stood holding my hand, waiting for me to agree with him. It would be so easy to say, "Yes, I see, you're right." Instead I said, "I'm still trying to sort things out in my head." What a stupid thing to admit! Now he could just dismiss everything I'd said as the confused mumblings of a mixed-up kid.

But instead of turning away, he kept hold of my hand. "I do hope you'll try again with Alissa," he said. "Whatever it was you two quarreled about, I hope you can get past it."

"Um," I said, surprised. "But isn't she going to private school next year?"

He shook his head. "Not if I have anything to say about it. Which I do. Alissa needs to spend some time in the real world." He hesitated. "My friends assure me it's only natural for a middle schooler to be so self-centered and shallow. But then I meet someone like you. I truly hope you can rub off on my daughter."

I swallowed, feeling the heat rise in my face. "I'll try to hang out with Alissa," I said. And then I laughed. "I tell you what. I'll try to see if I can get her and my friend Jolene to like each other."

He shook my hand again. "Your friend Jolene?" His voice dipped into a growl. "She sounds formidable. The two of them, now there's a challenge worthy of you."

As I walked back across the dining room, reporters surrounded me, thrusting microphones at me. I took a breath and told them about being blindfolded and locked in the car, and about my prison hut, and how I tried to dig my way out and how I once took the dog and tried to run away. I said everyone had been very kind to me since my release.

And then it was the police, taking me carefully through every detail. My parents sat with me, silent, and my mother held my hand. I described Jackson's looks, the car, what I remembered of the road. When they started asking for every detail I could remember of my captivity, I started to shake, and my mother asked them to give me a break.

When the police were gone, she took both my hands. My father kept quiet as she spoke. "Nala, Kenya is a country trying to build a rule of law. People can't take the law into their own hands. This man was violent to you. He hurt you. He could have gotten angry and killed you."

"He wanted to help the children of Kenya," I said.

My father said, "The murderers of al-Shabaab also believe they are serving the people. These beliefs do not give them the right to be violent."

Jackson wasn't really violent, I thought. But then I remembered my whipping, and the long nights, and being so frightened I wet my pants.

My mother said, "It seems this Jackson fellow was willing to sacrifice you for the sake of the children of Kenya. Would he be willing to sacrifice himself?"

I thought of the deal I had tried to make with Mr. Bowen. How could I expect him to break into a new role if I couldn't? With my voice drying up, I said, "I think maybe Jackson would be willing to sacrifice his freedom." I looked at my mother's hand holding mine, and finally I raised my eyes to my mother's face. "And his real name is Amos."

thirty-one

*B*y the time the Kitale Club held our repeat family banquet that night, I think police all over the country were searching for a dairyman called Amos with a dead child named Esther. I had spent the afternoon swimming in the club pool, tossing a ball and playing Marco Polo with a bunch of kids while Daniel and Nick prowled around the periphery of the pool like guardian lions.

I sat at the head table with my family and Daniel and Mr. Bowen and a lady from Drossila's media outreach department. Her name was Judith Birimba, and she told me media outreach meant talking to reporters. The reporters sat crowded into two tables at the back, with their camera equipment perched near the podium.

The dinner was duck and rabbit, with potatoes and no ugali. I guess it was sort of too bad to keep people from their ugali, because I hardly touched my dinner anyway.

As people started their dessert, a messenger came in and whispered in Mr. Bowen's ear. Mr. Bowen nodded, folded his napkin, and stepped up to the podium, where he beckoned for me to join him. As I walked, the room broke out in clapping. I stood next to Mr. Bowen, and he took my hand, which I didn't like, and leaned in toward the microphone.

"We're here tonight to celebrate the rescue of our lost heroine," Mr. Bowen said. The crowd cheered, and I tried to be happy about that and ignore the feeling that Drossila was using me. *I'm using them too,* I told myself. *I just hope it works.*

But then Mr. Bowen gave me a smile that crinkled his eyes, so I knew the smile was real. He looked kind, maybe even proud of me, and he nodded at me before he turned back to the crowd. "I'm also here to tell you two more pieces of good news," Mr. Bowen said, and he raised the hand that held mine, so it felt like he was the referee congratulating me, a boxer, at the end of a fight. "I have just received word that Nala's kidnapper has been captured."

My knees buckled. Mr. Bowen's arm held me up. People cheered and clapped, but my throat felt tight and my eyes were hot. I thought the clapping sounded sad.

Mr. Bowen waited until the room was quiet before he continued. "And finally, to honor Nala's courage, I am announcing tonight the establishment of a foundation to help all Kenyan people get the medicines, the repellants, the mosquito nets they need to fight malaria, all at cost, which means for only what it costs us to make the medicines. Soon we'll try to extend the program to other diseases as well." Mr. Bowen let my hand go, and I gripped the edge of his podium to support myself. I sought out Daniel's face in the crowd. He stood by his seat, cheering.

Mr. Bowen said, "This foundation will be funded with an initial donation of ten million dollars from Drossila Pharmaceuticals and five million dollars from the Bowen family. The name of the foundation will be the Lioness Foundation, and Nala Simiyu will be an honorary trustee."

Wild cheers and clapping. Mr. Bowen drew me toward the microphone. "Nala, you're an eloquent speaker. Do you have something to say?"

Not just butterflies, but giant bats fluttered in my stomach and chest. My tongue in my mouth grew enormous and dry. I looked out at the people, most of them clapping, some of them standing now and swaying. I looked at my family, Nick, my parents, Daniel who nodded at me, his beaded braids clattering against each other. I said, "Thank you. All of you." My voice cracked. I wanted to say they were all my family. Instead I said, "Come to Nairobi to help us. You matter. Your lives matter."

And then I fled back to my seat.

At about three in the morning, I crept into the bathroom with a sheet of hotel stationery and a pen. I closed the bathroom door so I wouldn't wake my mother, and I turned on the light. Crouching on the toilet seat, I began to write a letter. I had discussed it with Nick, and he said he thought it might help. *Dear judge,* I wrote. Then I crossed that out and started over.

Dear esteemed judge,

I am Nala Simiyu. I am writing to say that I think the man I knew as Jackson, who kidnapped me, did not have greedy motives. He was confused by grief over the loss of his child, and he wanted to save the lives of other children. He thought about everyone in Kenya, not just his own family or tribe.

He did not treat me badly. He fed me and gave me a good place to sleep. He let me help with the housework (crossed out) cuddle his baby and he loaned me a dog to keep me company.

I beg you to treat Mr. Jackson with mercy.

The letter was just a draft, and I would have to figure out where to send it, but writing it made me feel better. I folded the letter, left it on the counter, and crawled back into bed next to my mother.

The next day, we drove back toward Nairobi. Nick and Daniel took turns driving, and my parents sat in the back with me squished between them. They bickered a little, arguing about whether we should all crowd into my father's house in Nairobi with Alice and the kids, or whether we Americans should stay in a hotel.

"Did you even tell Nala?" my mother asked.

My father looked at me. "I hope it's all right. Alice and the kids are meeting us at Lake Nakuru."

"The flamingo lake?" I asked. Now that I had studied the map of Kenya, I knew Lake Nakuru was much too far from Kitale for Jackson-named-Amos, my kidnapper, the prisoner, the sacrificed one, ever to have taken me there.

"That's right, the flamingo lake. The younger children have never been there. But the main reason they're coming is they're so excited to see you they couldn't wait for you to get all the way home."

"Really?" I asked. I wanted to hold little Benjamin, to swing him, and I imagined the other kids swarming around me. We would put flamingo feathers in each other's hair. I asked, "Even Adam?"

My father laughed. "He wants to race you along the lakeside. I warn you, he's very fast."

I squeezed my father's hand. Some mixture of gladness and sorrow swelled insided me, making me feel younger and older at the same time. "Oh, he's not as fast as I am," I said. "I'm so fast I can fly."

About the Author

Pendred Noyce is a doctor and author of 11 books for young people. Penny has a diploma in tropical medicine and hygiene. She has worked to improve science education and afterschool science opportunities for young people nationwide.

"Bravo! A wonderful story, full of interesting science and important social issues."

– John Carlson, Higgins Professor of Molecular, Cellular, and Developmental Biology, Yale University.

How do you make science research, social justice, and history come alive for middle schoolers? You might not think of mosquitoes as the "secret sauce" but Pendred Noyce did. With a spirited main character, Nala Simiyu, Pendred writes a compelling and personal story that makes scientific research come alive so that you can't put the book down. She also weaves in social justice and social dynamics that kids in middle school navigate through. I enjoyed reading the story and would have loved to read aloud with my son when he was little. I encourage you to share a copy with a girl or boy in your life, with a library at your local public school, or a Free Library in your neighborhood.

– Linda Kekelis, CEO and Executive Director, Techbridge